PRAISE FOR THE MOTHERLESS CHILD PROJECT

"To say that The Motherless Child Project is a book about change and self-discovery would be doing it an injustice: it's so much more. Through Emily's actions readers are treated to insights on responsibility, community connections, and, ultimately, the lasting impact of decisions... Any teen reader looking for a powerful, compelling story—especially those who are motherless themselves, whatever the reason—will find The Motherless Child Project a powerful saga worthy of attention and acclaim." —D. Donovan, eBook Reviewer, Midwest Book Review

"My mother died when I was young (and so was she) so I was interested to learn what The Motherless Child Project was about... This book covered every emotion I ever felt, from the questioning of friends to the notable and always present absence of mother... Keeping it real, even though it's fiction, really makes the story work. The characters are well developed and easy to connect with. The story is written as if a teen wrote it... Th" —Carol Thompson for Reader's Favor

"Written with warmth, humor and honesty, with its remarkably realistic depiction of worst-case family court scenarios today, this book could become a game-changer." — Randy Kessler, national family law expert, law professor and author of Divorce: Protect Yourself, Your Kids and Your Future

"A gripping read about a young girl whose life changes on the bars of a song." — Amy Osmond Cook, Ph.D., communications professor and founder of DivorceSupportCenter.com

"A powerful exploration of the Family Court industry, The Motherless Child Project is also a full-on indictment of cultural attitudes toward women and children, and the most important work on Maternal Alienation to date... With [this book], McQueen and Karr emerge as the Dream Team of reality-based novels." — Jenna Brooks, award-winning author of October Snow and An Early Frost

"The Motherless Child Project is blasting the cover off thousands of secret, unwarranted child kidnappings in this country by the Family Court. McQueen and Karr's book reveals the little known harm perpetrated on American children by our courts with sharp vision, love and humor... They also provide the ever-elusive solution to a decades old problem of motherless children." — Malinda Sherwyn, mothers' and children's advocate

"I really think this book will lead children to search out the truth. The whole thing, twists and turns, finding little pieces of the puzzle, but unsure she wanted more, but deep inside she did....probably the very real feelings these children experience." — Rochelle Gelt, Amazon reviewer

HANGING ON BY MY FINGERNAILS: SURVIVING THE NEW DIVORCE GAMESMANSHIP, AND HOW A SCRATCH CAN LAND YOU IN JAIL
by Janie McQueen

"To the women who are victims of 'divorce gamesmanship': Look no further. This book will give you hope and courage, and real tools to break free." —Criminal defense attorney and FOX News Contributor Tamara Holder

"It's about time for a clear-eyed look at the divorce and custody industry. There are and have been plenty of books bemoaning the author's condition, along with various police and CPS agencies which failed to act; but McQueen does a fine job of sorting it out."—Familylawcourts.com

"This book is a MUST READ for ALL women. With more than fifty percent of marriages ending in divorce… what you don't know can seriously hurt you."—Deception and credibility expert Eyes for Lies[SM]

"Divorce is a game that has only gotten nastier as time has rolled on. 'Hanging On By My Fingernails: Surviving The New Divorce Gamesmanship, And How a Scratch Can Land You in Jail' is an exploration of the depths modern divorce legal battles can stoop to, leading to mutually assured destruction in many legal cases. A strong read for those who may be entering a nasty divorce battle in the future, especially geared towards women, 'Hanging On By My Fingernails' is a must for relationship and divorce library assortments."—Midwest Book Review

"This well-crafted, sometimes shocking book will let you in on tactics legal professionals have defended against for years. It's going to help legions of women avoid a very nasty trap." — Randall M. Kessler, Esq., national family law expert and law professor

THE MAGIC BOOKSHELF and THE NEW MAGIC BOOKSHELF: FINDING GREAT BOOKS YOUR CHILD WILL TREASURE FOREVER (10TH ANNIVERSARY EDITION)
by Janie McQueen

"Finding the right book for one's child is absolutely essential for promoting a lifelong love of reading. The New Magic Bookshelf: Finding Great Books Your Child Will Treasure Forever is a guide for parents and educators in matching children with the right books that will spark that love for literacy, and teach them that reading can be as fun as any toy or video game... The New Magic Bookshelf is a solid acquisition for anyone seeking to promote literacy in their own or others' children." —Midwest Book Review

"Adults often forget the strong connection between these two skills [reading and writing]. One naturally leads to the other. And parents and guardians can do more than they might think to encourage the reading-writing link." —Los Angeles Times Book Review

"An outstanding resource for parents, teachers and others who care about the reading life of a child." —Bella Online

The Motherless Child Project

Janie McQueen & Robin Karr

BURNING SAGE
ATLANTA

Copyright © 2014 by Janie McQueen and Robin Karr
www.themotherlesschildproject.com

All rights reserved. No part of this publication may be reproduced, stored in a retrieval system, or transmitted in any form or by any means, electronic, mechanical, photocopying, recording, or otherwise, without written permission of the publisher. For information regarding permission, contact Burning Sage Publishing House through the project website at www.themotherlesschildproject.com/

First Edition.

This is a work of fiction. All of the characters, names, incidents, organizations, and dialogue in this novel are either the product of the authors' imaginations or are used fictitiously.

Printed in the United states of America
ISBN-13: 978-0981611440
Library of Congress Control Number: 2014921743

Publisher's Cataloging-in-Publication data

McQueen, Janie Brooks.
   The Motherless child project / Janie McQueen ; Robin Karr.
   p. cm.
   ISBN 978-0981611440
   Summary : A young girl's sense of displacement is heightened when an Internet project leads her to seriously question her mother's absence from her life.

[1. Mothers and daughters --Fiction. 2. Fathers and daughters --Fiction. 3. Families --Fiction. 4. Secrets --Fiction. 5. Internet --Fiction.] I. Karr, Robin. II. Title.

PZ8.M1866 Mo 2015
[Fic] --dc23
         2014921743

For Christopher, Matthew and Laura
—R.K.

For Riley, Thomas, Sophia and John
—J.M.

Contents

Almost Gone   1
1 Motherless Child   5
2 Spiritual   19
3 Community   31
4 Little Closer   53
5 Messages   71
6 Bright   87
7 Threshold   99
8 BostonBaked   113
9 Threads   133
10 Baby Things   149
11 Hidden Words   163
12 Patterns   177
13 Snapshots   197
14 Ghost   217
15 Log-Off   231
16 Names   243
Shout   271

The Motherless Child Project

Footfalls echo in the memory

Down the passage which we did not take

Towards the door we never opened

Into the rose-garden. My words echo

Thus, in your mind.

                      But to what purpose

Disturbing the dust on a bowl of rose-leaves

I do not know.

                        —T.S. Eliot, from *The Four Quartets*

Almost Gone

I try to pull myself through the water, but my arms slice at nothing, as if striking air. I'm sinking, falling—or rising?—through soft, green space. I can't propel my body in the direction I think is up. Shadows and beams move and glow from all directions, confusing me. My eyes are open—there's no chlorine sting—but I'm lost.

Dusky shapes shift slowly before me, making delicate lacy patterns like fine branches of trees. Are they the real trees though? Or do I only see their ghostly silhouettes on the bottom?

I taste a tinge of salt and press my lips together so no water can enter my mouth.

Angry echoes volley back and forth from somewhere; not far. They bounce about me, hollow—not real words anymore—and I'm glad of that.

My lungs are burning and my chest is cramping up. Fiercely, I try to paddle while cupping my hands like Lee, my old swim teacher, taught me. Where is the air? Where is up? Ice cream scoops. Strawberry, chocolate. Scoop, scoop.

I'm a half-second from sheer panic.

I heard somewhere that drowning is a euphoric experience; not like it would seem—slow suffocation by water. If this is happening—if I'm drowning—I need to get to the good part if there is one. My lungs are screaming. And, it's terrible to know I cannot breathe.

Wild splashing; yelling—it's closer and louder. I turn to the sound. I flail towards it. A pair of long shadows hurtles towards me. Is my mind playing tricks? Is this the euphoria part? Is it?

"Emily Amber!" My name sounds like its coming from far, far away—from another world. Another time.

"Ember!" It's my brother Nick. He's the only one in my family who calls me that. Suddenly, though my lungs feel about to burst, I sense I have a chance. But I'm not sure I want to go back. Maybe the worst is over. Maybe I'm about to get to the feel-good part about drowning. Maybe I'll see a heavenly light from somewhere down here and magically move towards it—towards someone I really want to see.

Someone has my arms—firm—and is swimming furiously with me.

Do I want to go back up to that life?

After all, it's one big giant lie.

1

Motherless Child

Up or down? Even on dry ground, moving through my days, I'm not sure where I'm headed. To safety? Fresh air? More insanity? More excruciating places where I need to breathe, but can't?

Believe it or not, there are still times I feel like I'm about to suffocate, even when there's plenty of good air around. You can actually drown on land. It's called "dry drowning." I looked it up.

When I near drowned that time, even with the awful raw burning in my chest and my lungs threatening to burst if I was under for another split-second, I felt a lightness in my head like a suspension between life and death. Sometimes I wish I could feel like that again—drifting... in the in-between. Between not-knowing and knowing.

The knowing part has gotten me into a lot of trouble. I mean *a lot*. Enough trouble for a lifetime and maybe even more. My shrink, who I have to go see twice a week since I near-drowned, after they finally let me out of that hellhole in Columbia, says I have to catch up to this knowing because I was raised on a steady diet of lies.

And to think this insanely scary, suffocating stuff all began with something ridiculously small. In retrospect, I mean it was small. But I've learned that even the smallest problem—if you try too hard to solve it or take it too far—can swing your whole life around, turn it upside down and dump you out into a place you don't even recognize.

In the days of not-knowing, however, a fashion crisis was one of the worst things I could imagine, next to not losing five pounds before yearbook pictures. So maybe it's not that unusual that all this began something as seemingly harmless as a *dress*. Or, rather, the lack of one.

The dress was for my older cousin Jilly's wedding. I suspected a rush situation, given the short notice and obvious lack of formality. Where we live, most wedding invitations are crisp, creamy numbers stuffed with cards of different sizes and purposes, embossed in elegant script and addressed by real calligraphers.

Jilly's invitation was an Evite.

Leave it to cousin Jilly to add a special perk, or problem, depending on how you look at it. She wanted me to be one of her bridesmaids. "Mom's letting Uncle Jon know all about it," she'd P.S.'d, referring to my dad. "But I wanted to tell you myself."

Jilly's mother is Dad's sister Margot. They live Upstate. South Carolina is a small state, but the Upstate and the mid portion, which is called the Pee Dee, are totally different from the Lowcountry, where I've always lived.

My part of the state is green, wet, and humid. The salted-marsh air just hangs in space. You can feel yourself walk through it.

The Pee Dee is hot, flat, and boring, but at least it has the prettiest foliage and flowers.

As for the Upstate: It's red. Red skies, red clay and squishy red mud between my toes at the bottom of Lake Hartwell, where I'll wade around to cool off but never go in past mid-calf, where I can see. The murky water swirls with silt and silver-slimy fish that brush against my legs.

But Jilly is there, and that makes it worth it.

Anyway, as soon as I got the Evite, I immediately messaged Jilly:

What should I wear? R the bridesmaids wearing matching dresses?

I could already feel the anxiety creeping up the back of my neck.

No time. Just wear something that goes with lilac. Carly and I found these adorbs dresses for Tabitha & Tiffany at Carter's outlet.

Carly is Jilly's sister, and Tabitha and Tiffany are Carly's four-year-old twins.

Jilly pinged a pic of two identical dresses, more lavender than lilac in my opinion. They were white collared with smocked bodices, still stiff and tagged like paper-doll clothes on the pink and cream carpeting in Jilly's room.

I instantly knew finding something that remotely went with them, for someone over the age of nine anyway, was going to be a mega-challenge.

Finding something that *fit* was going to ratchet it up another notch. I was in between sizes, my current size 4, and the size 2 I wanted to be.

Jilly messaged:

U OK with this?

I'd been Googling "Colors That Go With Lavender."

Sorry, was thinking. I'll find something gr8!!

I hoped my message sounded more upbeat than the situation indicated. Jilly had enough to worry about on her end, pulling her wedding together so fast and all.

Still, fashion emergencies are not something I'm cool with. Matching a kid's springtime color in winter? Now, that's downright horrifying.

So I did what I do before pure fashion terror sets in and gets the better of me. I set out for Thrift-Eze in the ancient silver Volvo my brother Nick and I share. Thrift-Eze is a musty old second-hand store on King Street. I love to find stuff with possibilities—discarded things I can make new. Most things there seem out of place in one way or another but have potential, you know? Even though everyone else I know shops at mall stores or boutiques or online, I like the idea of giving things a second chance.

I unrealistically hoped for something pastel mixed in with all the wool and corduroy.

However, once I'd sifted through the merchandise twice, including the Last Chance rack, I felt like I was positively drowning in horrible clothing. Seriously, it was like trying to swim in ugly.

Maggie, the new store manager, must have quite an eye because she left the picked-over purse and wallet bin to come over to where I was now sitting forlornly on the floor.

I blinked up at her and saw she was holding a red patent leather clutch in one hand and a black knockoff Dooney & Bourke handbag in the other. Even though I didn't know her yet, I started blabbering, telling her about the wedding and how worried I was about finding something to wear. I added that not only did I need a dress, I needed it to be a particular color. Plus, I let her know in no uncertain terms that I intended to be a size 2 by the event date. It didn't matter to me that the wedding was only two weeks away. I'd gotten thinner faster.

"And I can't look like a total idiot," I finished, pausing for breath.

"Might have to get your mom involved with this one, girl," Maggie said, kneeling and regarding me with an expression of something between understanding and pity. I hate that look. But hey, I was a sixteen-year-old girl sitting on the dirty floor in the darkened dress section of a thrift store, surprised I didn't find the perfect dress.

"I think this occasion might call for a first-run sort of store, or maybe the Outlets for past season if you don't want to invest too much," Maggie added.

I'm used to people bringing up my mother from time to time—people who don't know us—but suddenly, surrounded by pitiful clothing that didn't have the tiniest flicker of possibility, I felt not only sad but utterly lost. I'd wished I'd had a mother to help. I needed someone to be in charge, and not in a pushy way, like Aunt Margot. I needed someone who knew what I was looking for—maybe more than I did myself. I'm not talking about a girlfriend like Sarah or Macy, who would mean well but would be as clueless as I was. No—I needed someone who could pull something amazing out of a forgotten cedar chest or maybe an armoire that lingered in some locked room. I could picture something long past its day, but which could be made over with a little ingenuity, a sharp eye, and a tuck here and there.

Really, I knew this was impossible, and not because I didn't live in an English novel or something. My mother wasn't around. She never had been around. She'd been a ghost—a mystery—my whole life.

Pretty weird, right? I suddenly found myself wishing for a basically nonexistent person to save me at that moment. It's not as if I didn't have any help. The store clerk, Maggie, was full of suggestions, but it wasn't the same as having a mom to help.

"I guess I'll check the mall," I said to Maggie, pulling myself up off the floor by the metal rack frame. I brushed off the seat of my burgundy skinny jeans and smoothed my yellow vintage mohair sweater over them. Maybe, I'd search online to see if I could get something in the mail in time.

"Good luck," Maggie said, waving the faux Dooney & Bourke. "You can always bring what you find to wear to the wedding here to resell when you're done with it."

I bought the red patent leather clutch Maggie had been holding and got in the Volvo. Driving home listening to Martina McBride sing *Teenage Daughters*, I felt deflated. All I had left to consult was the closest thing I had to a mom. My oldest brother Jon's girlfriend Ashley would have to do.

"Aw, Emily Amber," Ashley said. "Your first time in a wedding party, and you want me to be your stylist."

See? She's just like that. Give her a swipe of lipstick and she'll take the whole tube.

She plopped next to me on our ratty blue sofa—heaven knows why we keep it, but Dad argues it's "broken in"—and hugged me in a fog of Forbidden Euphoria. I stared at her, taking in the smoky eyes under her black London Lashes. My brother Nick and I call her "Lashley" behind her back.

"Actually, it's my second wedding party," I corrected. I'd been a junior bridesmaid in Carly's wedding five years ago.

"So. What look are we going for? Romantic? Edgy-chic?" Ashley chirped as I edged to the end of the sofa, pretending to read Dad's *Garden & Gun* magazine. "Cute guys," she said, looking over my shoulder at a black and white Brooks Brothers ad. "Boring clothes though."

I told Ashley my only official guideline was something that matched lavender, and showed her the pic of the little girls' dresses on my cell. Then I added my personal requirement that it be a size 2.

"Emily Amber, you're pretty thin as it is," Ashley said, squinting at me so her lashes looked perilously close to sticking together.

"And the dress will be out of season I'm sure, but it has to be at least cute, because I don't want to look ridiculous," I finished.

Ashley leaned back into the sofa cushion, considering as she picked at the leaking stuffing with a blue metallic fingernail. As silly and overdone as she comes across sometimes, she's not stupid. She's studying nursing at the Medical University of South Carolina and stays at the top of her class. Besides, I was desperate.

"It's too bad she didn't give you any time to speak of," Ashley mused. "But it doesn't seem like... *she has the luxury of time.*" She said the latter part in a demure whisper.

"Um, no it doesn't." I was far more worried about my appearance than I was about Jilly being pregnant.

"We need some inspiration," Ashley declared. "How about 1960s cool? Think *Mad Men*, seventh season.

Oh man, I wish there was some place to get a Pucci dress around here. You're skinny and you seem taller than you are. You could *so* pull off Pucci. We could try eBay."

"Um, I'm not sure we have time for that," I said.

Ashley quickly shook her head like she was throwing off a gnat. "No. 'Course not. Well, you could wear something of mine. But most everything I have is black. Still, I'm loving this retro thing. Hey, let's get some inspiration. Are there any old wedding pictures around here? Maybe your parents'?" Instantly Ashley clapped her hand over her mouth. "Oops, I'm sorry!"

In my house, no one talks about anything concerning my mother—not Dad, nor Jon, Nick, nor me. Ashley comes from a family of five kids and married parents, so she brings it up accidentally every now and then. She can't help it. I guess it's reasonable to her, but Jon shushes her with a menacing look and probably a pinch or a kick under the table. Who knows what he says or does to her later? She just can't seem to get the message that our mother is a taboo topic.

You're probably wondering why it's taboo.

I can't—couldn't—answer that. The best way I can explain it is like this: When it's a fact of your life your mother is MIA, and you know you'll never get anywhere by asking where she is because you've tried numerous times with bad-to-worse results, you just move on with your life. What else can you do?

I stood up, trying to think of a way to bail myself out of the conversation. "You know what? I'm going to re-check my closet for something I might can wear. There's got to be something."

I ran three steps at a time upstairs, a habit I've never bothered to kick. It gets me away from situations that have no possibility of a good outcome.

2

Spiritual

After the Thrift-Eze meltdown, reminders that I didn't have a mom seemed to start popping up everywhere.

It's not like I couldn't have done with a mom's touch lots of times growing up. Like Halloween. Dad always got us those cheap store-bought costumes from Wal-Mart or Party Town. He didn't know any better, but I knew they were tacky even when I was six. So I came up with costumes on my own.

My all-time best costume started with an old red bonnet I used to play dress-up. I found an empty moving box in the garage and sawed a big square in the front using heaven knows what. With a box of raisins as a model, I painted the moving box to look as much like it as I could. I poked my head through the hole and went to my school carnival as the Sun Bonnet Girl. I'd even curled my hair into ringlets—though mine is brown instead of blond—and brushed it into a low side ponytail like hers and tied it with a wide red grosgrain ribbon. I won the prize for "Most Creative."

Muffins with Mom events growing up weren't that big a deal either. Dad would come and be so funny and fascinating that all the other moms ignored their own kids. There always seemed to be another kid in the class with a single dad.

There were only vague reminders that I didn't have a mother. Until an old gospel song changed all that.

Except this song wasn't just in my ear. It filled the whole sanctuary of my friend Macy's church and literally shook the wood-panel walls. The fact that someone around my age sang it made it all the more surreal.

Spiritual

I usually go along with Macy on Sunday mornings if I stay overnight. My family belongs to St. Paul's, an Episcopal church downtown, where Dad is on the men's prayer breakfast committee and A Father's Promise and lots of other groups. But I prefer hearing the music and the Morning Message at Cross Path Community Church instead of standing up and reciting and sitting down and standing up again for an hour, and then waiting around for Dad to finish his church business before we go to the country club for lunch.

Harbour Point might have the killer buffet, but I still prefer coffee and Faith Foods donuts in the Cross Path reception hall.

Macy's family is rich. Her dad founded Faith Foods, and I was glad they didn't go to a stuffy church like mine. Cross Path strives to be accessible to everyone which I guess is why I like it.

Macy sings in the Cross Path Praise Choir. That's another huge draw—they're the best church choir in the Lowcountry, maybe even the state. While Macy's up in

Spiritual

the choir loft, sometimes I sit with her parents—who are supremely cool—but usually I find somewhere to sit up in the balcony. Even though I'm technically surrounded by people, church gives me a rare opportunity to just *be*, with nothing more required of me. I guess you could say church is the place I feel safest, next to my bedroom.

Now even in my "safe" places, I can no longer be one hundred percent sure I'm safe anymore.

A few minutes before I heard The Song That Changed Everything, I was sitting in a back-balcony seat against the wall, mulling over Jilly's wedding the previous weekend. On the drive Upstate, Dad had gotten on this rant about people marrying so young.

"They have their whole lives to settle down. If Jilly insists on having a baby, I don't know why she just doesn't adopt it out. There are... *programs* for unwed mothers. They don't even call them 'unwed' anymore since a wedding isn't even expected! I don't know who pressed them into getting *married*. Margot, I guess. Poor guy is probably on a ledge right now."

Spiritual

"Jilly seems to really want the baby. I think she's glad her boyfriend wants to get married," I ventured, knowing Dad would have a retort for this, but that I was too old for him to swat from the front seat. Still, on reflex, I nestled against the bridesmaid outfit I'd managed to pull together, which hung beside me still draped in its filmy dry-cleaner bag. I'd ended up borrowing one of Ashley's old dresses, one I couldn't possibly envision her ever having worn. It was a summery white eyelet number with cap sleeves and a sash of yellow daisy appliques, which we'd replaced with a length of lavender satin we found at Jo-Ann Fabrics.

"Honey, no boyfriend wants to get married," Dad said, throwing a smirk at me across his headrest. Jon snickered next to him. Nick just looked plain pissed.

Unlike Macy's church, which was large, noisy, and multiethnic, Jilly's was small, white, and Presbyterian. When we arrived at Aunt Margot's before the wedding, I was instantly relieved to see everyone wearing similarly desperate outfits. Even if I looked more like I should be scattering rose petals in the aisle with Tabitha and Tiffany instead of standing with the other bridesmaids, I looked okay in comparison.

Jilly looked gorgeous and thrilled in blush-colored satin that tastefully ruched at the waist. Some hair artist had woven her dark blond hair into an impressive array of loops and coils and creamy white roses and baby's breath. I had to agree with the discreet wedding description Aunt Margot proudly showed me, which she'd sent to the local paper in advance: *The bride looked radiantly aglow.*

I felt pleased for Jilly. At two years older than me—Nick's age—she had always made me feel everything was going to be okay. She'd always "broken the ice" for me like a sister would. She got her ears pierced first, developed breasts first, got her period first, started dating boys first, did all the "firsts" so I didn't feel so self-conscious when I got around to them. (Now she had the pregnant part in the can too—a mite earlier

Spiritual

than I would choose. Not that she probably chose it exactly.)

I was pondering the many firsts somebody can have until Sylvia, who is the closest thing Cross Path Community Church has to a pastor, snapped me out of my thoughts. "We have an extraordinary musical visitor, a young singer named Chloe Martin. Chloe has come up from Savannah to participate in the Lowcountry Choral Festival, and she's staying with the Marsh family. We're so pleased to have her with us today, singing a piece she performed at the festival yesterday."

The Cross Path Choir sings everything from traditional hymns to contemporary tunes, like you hear on the radio—except the songs are about God and Jesus, of course. But this one was different. It was an old African-American spiritual, according to the church bulletin.

The choir has a principal soloist, Bernadette Coolidge, who sounds like she could be on The Voice, or at least on the radio. It was really weird to see someone

Spiritual

different—a girl about my age behind the center microphone.

Then she sang, in a clear and confident voice, words that seemed to come from an ancient place:

Sometimes I feel like a motherless child
Sometimes I feel like a motherless child
Sometimes I feel like a motherless child
A long ways from home

Sometimes I feel like I'm almost gone
Sometimes I feel like I'm almost gone
Sometimes I feel like I'm almost gone
A long ways from home

Sometimes I wish that I could fly
Like a bird up in the sky
Sometimes I wish that I could fly
Like a bird up in the sky
Sometimes I wish that I could fly

Spiritual

Little closer to my home

I found myself gripping my armrests. Goosebumps pricked my forearms as the rest of the choir joined in:

Motherless children have a really hard time
Sometimes, sometimes, sometimes, sometimes
So far, so far, so far, so far
Mama, from you
So far

I felt hot tears start to well. They brimmed over, slid down my cheeks and plopped like fat raindrops onto my program. I willed them to stop, but they wouldn't. Fiercely hoping no one would notice me, I slunk down the side stairs. I tried to hide my burning face behind my bulletin.

The ladies' room off the main lobby was occupied only by a small strawberry blond-haired girl perched on

Spiritual

a black rubber stool. At first, I thought she was a military kid. She looked out of place with bangs and straight waist-length hair instead of the uniform chin-length bob most little girls around here wear. And rather than a smocked bishop dress and gigantic grosgrain bow, she wore a blue satin dress-up Cinderella dress, a pair of tiny plastic kitten heels, and a nametag hastily printed in red: DESIREE.

It occurred to me that she might be the little sister of the guest soloist from Savannah. They had the same hair.

I waited as she washed her hands carefully, then held each wet finger one by one under the dryer, which seemed to fascinate her. Her sparkly fingernails matched her dress. She seemed not to notice me the whole while.

After she left in her little cloud of tulle, I shut myself into a stall, sat on the edge of the toilet, and did three *pranayama* sequences, trying to focus on my breathing—in, two, three, four, out, two, three, four. Still, that song was already beginning to haunt me. It seemed

Spiritual

to echo off the drab green concrete-block walls of the bathroom and reach over into my stall:

True believer... A long ways from home.

I managed to dry up and cool down by the time Macy texted me from the choir room. It was her turn to be "robe keeper." This was a rotating position that entailed making sure everyone's choral attire got put away neatly after the service and that none smelled offensive after the wearers rocked out in the sanctuary. So fortunately, she hadn't missed me.

But when we met up outside the education building in the harsh noonday sunlight, I could tell she was trying to figure out what was off about me. I tried to act normal. "Let's go get some coffee," I said. "Hey, do you ever see Doug Arnold around here anymore?" Doug is a champion swimmer who'd withdrawn from our high school to homeschool and train full-time.

Still, that song was spooling in my head:

Spiritual

Sometimes I feel like a motherless child...

A long ways from home.

So far, so far, so far…

3

Community

I just couldn't seem to shake that song. It had become a mantra of sorts. It haunted me during ordinarily quiet times like yoga and wedged its way into my studying the second my mind wandered a little.

I was humming it in Life Skills when the deep voice of my teacher, Mr. Neil, cut in. Even though I'd had him as a teacher for two years, it was always startling to hear that booming tone come out of such an average-looking person. You know how people call a dull person *vanilla*? After much thought, I've decided Mr. Neil is *khaki*.

Until he opens his mouth.

"What makes you feel unique?"

Startled silent, I sneaked a look around to see if Mr. Neil meant just me.

"What sets you apart from others?" he went on.

Mr. Neil can shift from totally informal to military-stern in a snap. He graduated from The Citadel and went straight into the Marines. After he was honorably discharged because of some injury, he'd decided to teach. Despite his usual attention-getting style, this was a weird tack. Everyone automatically started shuffling and straightening in their seats.

Mr. Neil smiled and picked up a green whiteboard marker. We all knew a smile meant he was about to throw a curve ball. Turning to the board, he wrote:

I feel like the only one who…

Then below that, he made a list:

Community

Situation

Preferences

Family

Ethnic group

Physical traits

Personal style

Personality

Tastes

Beliefs

Hobbies

"If we have to pick just one of those, I'm going to need to consult my shrink," Mike Livingston cracked. "It's going to be tough to choose." His friends snickered.

"Whatever it takes," Mr. Neil said, ignoring the joke. He turned back to the class, leaned against his desk, and twiddled the marker in his stumpy fingers like a cigar. I noticed the wide gold wedding band that was normally on his left hand had been replaced with a fishbelly-white stripe of skin.

Community

"We're going to spend the next quarter on this project, wrapping up around Easter. So think hard and think deep about your topic, because you'll be living with it *every single day*. That being said, I hope you not only choose something liveable, but a topic that is challenging while true to yourself. This is an opportunity for real growth here. What makes *you* feel like the only one?"

Sarah Goddard, who I've known forever and sat by me in Life Skills, raised her hand. She'd started wearing this enormous mood ring that, strangely, seemed to be always deep blue, which was supposed to mean you were sublimely happy. I will give Sarah that she tried very hard to be happy—but she just hadn't quite gotten there yet.

"Yes, Miss Goddard?"

"Can our difference be about food preference?" Sarah asked. Some kids tittered.

I knew what her topic was going to be because she'd recently switched to a vegan diet. Her mother had

Community

been diagnosed with breast cancer two years ago. Now that she was in remission, the whole Goddard family had adopted a plant-based lifestyle. They'd even started a campaign to convert local homes to solar energy. Which is very tricky in a community built just barely after the Civil War. The *Post and Courier* was practically camped out on their front steps, waiting for the Board of Architectural Review to get sufficiently nervous to spark a fight.

"Being a vegan makes you feel really great." Sarah swiveled in her seat to address the whole class. "But being a vegan is *hard*, socially, I mean. Like, when you're at someone's house and you can't eat anything they have, even if they made it especially for you. And, did you know that nothing in the cafeteria is one hundred percent vegan except for raw vegetables? And even those aren't organic. They've all been treated with chemicals." She waved the hand with the ring for emphasis.

Community

"That's why I wish other people would go vegan. I mean, apart from the obvious health and environmental benefits."

A smile twitched on Mr. Neil lips. "I can see how you would feel alone in this, especially around here, where it's all seafood and spare ribs," he said. "My daughter happens to be a vegetarian. I'll bet you'll find a good many other like-minded souls."

"But Mr. Neil, being vegan and vegetarian aren't the same. Although people always think so. See, vegetarians…"

She stopped, frowning in frustration as Mr. Neil turned back to the whiteboard and jotted an Internet address: /theidentityproject/charlestonhigh.org.

"Don't worry," I whispered to her. "You'll get the perfect chance to educate people with your project." I'd had to have proper vegan schooling from Sarah myself.

"Each of you will create your own Internet community." Mr. Neil underlined the URL. "Only students in participating schools will have access to the

Community

project. But there are quite a few signed up, all across the country, from Washington state to Florida, from Maine to California. You might discover others are more like you than you think, even when they seem to live a world away.

"In addition, you will be required to join at least one other community. In this way, all the students participating will be able to cross-pollinate and encourage membership."

"Mr. Neil," Mike called out again. "There's a ton of fakes on the Internet. How will we know the other people are for real?"

"How will they know you're for real?" Mr. Neil shot back, and everyone laughed. "Actually, that's an excellent question. Teachers and other faculty members will have access to the communities. There'll be an honor code too. But we'll try to let you reach out in your own ways as long as you follow the guidelines. We're going to go over them, but they're all there on the website. And you can always ask or message me if you need clarification or have any problems."

"In real life, you never know the reason behind what people are doing, either." This was my practical friend Macy. "Like, a guy might join a choir because he likes a certain girl, not because he necessarily likes to sing."

Well, that was obvious. For years, Macy had waited for totally-taken Sam Collins to have some kind of spiritual—if not romantic—epiphany and magically appear next to her in the choir loft.

I glanced over at Sarah, who was frowning as she typed in the website address on her iPad. I knew she was worried about what her mother would say about the project. It was always interesting to see how Sarah's mom would react to something new. She's always been extremely strict. Since her cancer diagnosis and recovery, she'd given the term "Helicopter Parent" new meaning.

But at least she was there. And even if she cared too much, she cared.

Community

"Good heavens, Emily Amber, you are totally in space," Macy said at lunch, setting her blue plastic tray on the table Sarah and I had scoped out in the back corner of the cafeteria.

Sarah had brought her own vegan meal as usual. I always packed my own lunch too, because the school lunch is not only gross, it's fattening and has who knows what in it: GMOs and sodium and probably worse. Today I'd brought chicken salad I'd made with a tin of Chik-Lite and low-fat mayo on a bed of lettuce. With the added carrot strips and a pear, it seemed a perfectly balanced meal. As I unpacked it, I was pleased to note it almost looked like one of those "serving suggestions" I'm always trying to copy.

My mind had been stuck on the Life Skills project ever since class that morning. This was unusual, and, as usual, Macy had noticed. "Earth to Emily Amber," she sing-songed.

Community

"Oh. I guess I'm thinking about the project," I said.

"You guys look like you brought some real lunches today, not just rabbit food," Macy observed, wrinkling her nose at the slice of square cheese pizza in front of her, which already looked congealed and cold. I've never understood why she chooses to consume the school lunch every day when her dad owns the most delicious food business in the world. When I ask her, she says she gets tired of frozen food every day. Like school food isn't frozen?

Maybe she's making a personal statement. Who knows?

"You could make that vegan," Sarah said to me as she carefully arranged her lunch items on the bamboo plate she'd brought from home. "Except with no chicken. And you could make it a sandwich if the bread doesn't have any dairy ingredients in it."

"What's the point of making chicken salad without chicken?" Macy asked.

Community

"You could substitute with *tofu-ken*," Sarah said with a tinge of exasperation in her voice. This is why she usually addresses her suggestions only to me. Macy points out the holes in things. "It's tofu seasoned to taste like chicken."

Macy arched an eyebrow and said, "Sarah, you're working awfully hard to find stuff that tastes like meat. You think it'd be easier to eat—oh, I don't know—meat?"

Sarah ignored her and went back to appraising her lunch.

I tried not to laugh by taking a bite of chicken salad. It was pretty tasty, if I did say so myself. I'd added curry to it as suggested by the *Lo-Fat and Flavorful* cooking and dieting blog I follow. A teaspoon of curry equals seven calories, but I instantly decided it was worth it.

"So what are you guys thinking about for the project?" Sarah asked. "My mom..."

Community

She didn't have to finish: Macy and I knew how her mom was. Sarah sighed and dug into her guacamole with a whole-wheat cracker.

"The Internet is never going away," Macy pointed out. "Even if it does, it'll just... morph... and become something else."

"I can't do anything about what my mom thinks," Sarah declared, "and I'm not fighting her anymore. Especially after what she's been through. Besides, there's an alternative project that's not online. I asked Mr. Neil after class."

"Well, I'm using the 'net. I doubt I'll find any other teen atheists around this Bible Belt." Macy pushed away her pizza and looked at me. "Okay. I give in. Can I try that?"

I spooned a decent dollop of chicken salad onto Macy's plate, pleased with the opportunity to cut down my portion in the name of charity. "Try 'Praise Singers Who Don't Believe in God.' You could actually *be* the only one."

Community

"Yeah," Macy agreed and took a big bite, nodding vigorously as she chewed. "Emily Amber," she said through her mouthful, "this is... better than most of your low-cal stuff." She swallowed. "Bring me some tomorrow if there's any left? I start hunting atheists tonight. That'll at least give me a consolation prize to look forward to."

"Well, if you don't find any, you can start a community of people who always buy the school lunch, but never finish it and end up bumming off healthy people's rabbit food." I winked, and she threw me a fake scowl.

After school, I was starving. I scooped a small mound of my chicken salad for a snack, reasoning that I'd given nearly half my serving to Macy at lunch. I left enough for the sandwich I'd promised her. I opened a column of Saltines, carefully counted out ten, poured a glass of Diet Dr. Pepper in one of Dad's highball glasses, and balanced everything on a plastic tray with a pastel

Community

picture of Rainbow Row. That's a famous street in Charleston. Shifting my backpack so I wouldn't spill everything, I went upstairs to my room.

I set the tray on my bedside table, changed out my skinny jeans for my gray yoga pants and pulled my laptop from under the bed. I fished my Life Skills notebook out of my backpack—Jon had sat on my new iTablet at Christmas— to get the web URL for the project and logged on.

All the way home, my mind was stuck on the community project. Designing my home page was going to be the easy part: I'd created tons of blogs, even though I always lost steam after about the second post. It's a good thing you can't be arrested for blog abandonment. I'm sure I'd be put away for quite a while for all those posts floating around, lost and bloggerless in the ether.

Drawing my legs up in the lotus position, I munched crackers on auto-pilot as I located my favorite website-builder, created a new login and a password and

Community

connected it to the project website as instructed. The next step was to choose an online name for myself.

That came easily enough too—EMBER, I typed.

"Ember" is Nick's, uh, nickname for me. It's obviously just a combination of my two names, but I've always felt proud that Nick thought it up just for me. He's only twenty-two months older than I am, but I've always looked up to him more than anyone around me. He's always seemed wise, intense, but with a wicked sense of humor too.

I like the nickname's fiery implications, too. I don't think I'm "fiery" per se, but I do have a spark, like an ember. See? Maybe it was cheesy for an online persona, but I had to come up with something. And it had real meaning, unlike those stupid random online name generators, where I'd always gotten something idiotic like "RestlessAirman" or "FunkyLobster." Those are definitely not cool.

My fingers tingled, itching to create. I love formatting; I love picking different styles and deciding what works and what doesn't. I might change a design twenty times before I'm completely satisfied.

Playing with themes, colors, and fonts is also excellent for avoiding actually getting down to work. As I tinkered, I reminded myself I needed a workable topic.

At the back of my mind was the whisper of an idea. It didn't have a definite shape yet, but I had the familiar feeling I was on the verge of a revelation.

I stalled for time, fiddling with format and color combinations until Jon yelled that supper was ready. Tuesday was Jon's cook night. He was into stir-fry lately, which was getting a little boring but was an enormous improvement. Plus, it was usually low-cal. Pre-Ashley, he'd always just boiled hotdogs. It was a special treat if he came up with a can of chili to go on them. He never followed my suggestions, like wrapping the hotdogs in crescent rolls or even just chopping them up with baked beans once in a while. I did throw some appreciation Ashley's way for expanding his culinary horizons just a tad.

Community

After supper, I finished my other homework, then Skyped Sarah and Macy as a means of further procrastination.

Macy had clipped in a lime green hair extension since I'd seen her at school earlier. It was difficult to stand out in a sea of blue and white robes, so she'd decided to accent the only part of her that wasn't covered up—her head. She was experimenting with different looks. I knew she mainly wanted to stand out for Sam Collins.

She was nimbly weaving the extension into the rest of her hair with her slender cocoa-colored fingers as she talked.

"I've already been Googling teen atheists," she reported, "and so far no one else seems to go to church. Don't some of their parents make them go anyway? Am I being a hypocrite?" She hesitated. "But I really, really like to sing. And we're desperate for altos who can read sheet music. Some of the altos start singing the soprano part because they can't harmonize, or they go off on their own. It ruins the whole anthem!"

"Maybe you're not quite ready to be an atheist," I suggested. Macy frowned as she continued to finger-comb her hair, considering.

Sarah's mother had hit the ceiling as expected.

"She said she's calling the school tomorrow to protest about the project," Sarah moped. I idly wondered what color her mood ring turned for "depressed," but I didn't think it was a good time to ask, and I couldn't get a bead on it because she was flailing her hand around. Instead, I asked why her mother would do that—call the school I mean. Although, come to think of it, she did it all the time.

"She doesn't think it sounds safe."

"Didn't Mr. Neil say he'd make an alternative to doing an online project?" Macy asked, her face brightening suddenly. "Hmm." You could almost hear the synapses crackling in that head of hers.

Community

"Doesn't matter. She doesn't think anyone should do it at all," Sarah answered bleakly.

Mrs. Goddard was just like those meddling neighbor ladies on TV. If the perceived problem wasn't at school, she'd call wherever she thought it was. She'd always been this way, but her cancer diagnosis seemed to have focused her worries to a sharp point.

Nick's term for moms like Mrs. Goddard was "smothers." At least we didn't have one of those. Of course, we didn't have any mother, smother or otherwise.

Eventually, Macy and Sarah both had to go, and I reluctantly returned to my website. I did have a pretty cool design, nicely contrasting colors, cool turquoise and deep coral and an online name that actually meant something—to me anyway.

I reached in my nightstand for the vanilla lavender soy candle I keep in my bottom drawer for easy access when I do yoga or need to chill out. I rotate scents, but vanilla lavender is my favorite. The combination is

Community

supposed to calm you and bring back pleasant memories. I lit it with the Duck Dynasty Bic I'd stolen from Nick. The soy had melted down nearly to the bottom of the glass bowl, and I had to tilt it sharply to avoid burning my fingers. Absent-mindedly I flipped on my Internet streaming station, trying to summon the idea I could still feel lurking in the back of my mind.

There had to have been fifty or sixty songs on my "homework" playlist; however, about every fourth song that came up was a version of "Sometimes I Feel Like A Motherless Child." That's how many renditions I'd found. I'd begun collecting them right after hearing the song in Macy's church. I guess I thought making them into a soundtrack would get the song out of my head and confine it to a list.

What it actually did was add more *voices* singing the very same song through my head.

Right now, a female vocalist was singing the now intimately-familiar tune in a honey-rich voice—it rang clear even through the crackly background of an old recording. I began to listen more carefully.

> *Sometimes I wish that I could fly*
> *Like a bird in the sky…*
> *Little closer to home.*
> *True believer…*

I felt the prick of tears behind my eyes. *Emily Amber, you will not cry*, I told myself sternly.

I tried to correct my wayward emotions with reason. I was not "a long way from home," as the singer lamented. I was home right now, sitting cross-legged on my bed, palms up and resting on my knees, fingers curled in sideways okay signs. I silently regarded my bedroom walls, which were painted Honeysuckle, the 2013 Pantone "Color of the Year."

There it was! I too felt like a motherless child, while the singer only felt like one sometimes. I was one

Community

all of the time. I didn't know why it had become so important lately. It just was.

I snapped my right hand out of *Gyan Mudra* and struck a computer key to dismiss the screen saver. Up popped my community design. A style option I hadn't seen before leaped out at me: *Online message board*. I clicked on it.

Then automatically, I typed:

THE MOTHERLESS CHILD PROJECT

A COMMUNITY

BY EMBER

4

Little Closer

I located several general discussion leader-topic type questions on the Life Skills project site, and I entered them. Then, in a burst of inspiration, I decided to see if I could stream my personal Internet station onto my site.

I could. I decided to create a new station made up of all the Motherless Child song versions. I selected the versions I'd already culled for my homework soundtrack. But I found the number of others was considerable, from the earliest known recording by a group called the Fisk Jubilee Singers to Lena Horne to

Sinéad O'Connor, to Prince. For some reason, the version by Marian Anderson from the 1930s was my favorite so far. It sounded old-timey and crackly, but her rich contralto voice rang right through it. It seemed to transcend the recording itself and beam into the room.

It grabbed me by the heart.

I drew a few deep breaths and pressed *Publish*.

For a while, I sat and stared at my community, with its clean lines and nicely arranged boxes, bubbles, shapes, and text. I realized I should probably lead off with my own story—even if there wasn't much to tell. I posted on the welcome thread, careful to avoid textese:

WELCOME FROM EMBER: I was inspired to create this community because I heard the song "Sometimes I Feel Like A Motherless Child" at my friend's church. I don't have any information about my mother. It's not like I'm actually looking for her—I mean, she's like a ghost—but not having a mother makes me feel different. So, that's the project, and I decided to see if there are any other kids who feel like "motherless children." Thanks and I hope to hear from you! Ember.

It wasn't required, but I decided to upload the only good picture I believe has ever been taken of me. It was taken by this photographer who was visiting during Spoleto, an arts festival in Charleston, last year. I was standing by this kids' craft stand. There was the cutest little boy about three or four who goes to our church, who was mesmerized by a fan that generated bubbles. The photographer asked if he could take some pictures of us, promising to send prints, which he did.

I felt too tired to do any more, so I shut my laptop down, pulled my This Girl Hearts Country nightshirt over my yoga pants, and switched off the bedside light. I crawled underneath my black and white chevron print coverlet, wondering if I'd get any visitors to my community. I was beginning to worry that no one would understand my topic. Would I be sorry? Embarrassed? Would I be the only person in class who didn't get a bite?

Little Closer

It might make me feel more alone than ever. Well, I had time to change my mind and my topic.

The moon was on the full side. Its silvery fingers reached through my windows to the dark pink walls and stirred my room into a rosy bath. I let my consciousness drift. Ideas mixed with memories formed and switched like a dreamy slideshow in my head.

A scene from long ago floated into my mind's view. It was my seventh birthday and I was lying on my trundle bed playing a game connecting the dots on my green and yellow polka dot comforter. My face was sticky with tears. For my birthday that year, I'd wanted one of those cakes—you know the ones with a real plastic doll body and her flouncy skirt is the cake? Well, Dad had gotten me a circus cake from the Piggly Wiggly.

When I saw that evil-looking clown and the crude ringmaster with his whip and the sad, badly painted animal figures perched all over that thin sheet of white icing, I burst out crying. I raced up to my room and refused to leave for the rest of the day.

Little Closer

Everyone was beating on my door, trying to get me to come down and look at my presents: Dad, Nick, and even Jon. "Emily Amber, you come down right now," Dad ordered. "Come look at your presents. You're acting like an ingrate."

Fueled with a heady sense of birthday power and disregard for consequences, I'd refused. Dad could have broken down the door, of course, but he didn't. When everybody finally gave up and went away, I calmed down.

You know that fuzzy place between being awake and drifting off to sleep—like when you blow a soap bubble—and you can almost see something in it, something important? But if you reach out to touch it, to bring it closer—Pop! It vanishes more quickly than it appeared? Well, that's where I found myself.

I didn't know if I was drawing on some real recollection or not. But I conjured up a sort of angel with chestnut brown hair and grayish-green eyes, coloring similar to mine, and a smile that tells you everything will be okay. She drifted into the edge of my consciousness, much like Glinda the Good Witch floats into Munchkinland in her giant bubble.

Back then, I guess I thought she was an angel I imagined coming to greet me and make me happy on my birthday. Only now did I recognize her as a mother figure—someone who would know what kind of cake a little girl would want or what kind of dress would work for a challenging occasion.

I drifted deeper into another memory.

Nick and I were very little, maybe around five and seven. We'd been playing in a pile of autumn leaves in the backyard of Dad's parents, who lived Upstate. A delicious cool stung the air. I rolled over in the brittle leaves and asked Nick, "Why doesn't anyone talk about our mommy? Don't we have one?"

Even as a young kid, Nick had this kind of brooding intensity. Even as I worshiped him, I thought it scary. I never wanted to make him mad because he was the most important person in my entire world. While the people around me behaved unpredictably, Nick was steadfast and solid.

"I think we did," he answered slowly, lying back in the leaves and looking up as if searching for something in the naked branches overhead.

"Did she get sick and leave?" I pressed. I knew even then these questions were risky, but I really wanted to know. "Did she die?"

Nick had gotten up. I watched him, waiting, both dreading and craving the answer at the same time. Finally, he shook his head.

"Look, Emily Amber," he said—it was before he'd come up with "Ember"—"I'm working on knowing more. But we'll get in trouble if we ask about her, just like before."

I didn't remember "before." And at that moment, I'd been too frightened to ask Nick what he meant. But I'd taken his warning very much to heart. I never spoke to anyone about my mom again, at least in the form of a question. Few people asked about her. I got used to the way things were—had always been. Time passed.

Now the question I tried to suppress came back as I lay there in my bed watching those milky-pink moonbeams playing on the ceiling, near the place where I'd first imagined the angel lady. Dad and everyone else could enforce the silence about my mother all they wanted. It was normal for all of us, but it wasn't natural. It was a forced cool. Buttoned up. Hiding.

Why?

"Why are you staring at me, Ember?" Nick eyed me from across the breakfast table the next morning.

I hadn't realized I was staring; my mind was a buzzing hive of thoughts and questions, but I tried to focus on my usual routine.

Jon and Dad were in the kitchen too, getting coffee and arguing about the NFL game last night, something about whether a quarterback got "lucky" or if his offensive line saved him. Jon had graduated last spring, but he was still here for the time being, working at Second Chance Sports while he waited to hear about a football scholarship at Gardner-Webb. He hadn't made the cut first time around, but his counselors advised him to try again when he was a year older, but still not too old to be a freshman.

I can't understand for the life of me how sports could be important enough to stick around here unnecessarily. Although I hadn't had a chance to think much about college.

That morning, I knew there was no way anyone would know about my project—yet—but I already had serious jitters. I mechanically dropped a piece of multigrain bread into the toaster. When my bread popped up nice and brown, I attempted to apply the non-dairy Better Butter (Sarah's suggestion). It clung stubbornly to the bread in stiff, sticky clumps.

"Hey guys, check out this vegan butter. It's so much healthier than the sludgy stuff we've been eating." I closed my eyes and bit off a corner. It took a while to chew—I chased it down with a half-glass of vanilla almond milk.

"Yummy," I pronounced.

I looked up. Nick eyes narrowed in on me, in his "What's going on?" expression.

I knew I'd taken a huge step in a forbidden direction. It was as if, overnight, I'd traveled miles into the future. Nick had no way to know that, of course. Still, his trouble-detection skills were even sharper than Macy's.

I polished off most of the rest of my toast, more than I usually eat, mainly to have something to do. Then I stood up and tugged on my green hoodie, the only piece of clothing I own that I'm not allowed to alter because it's a school licensed item. Hoisting my backpack onto my shoulder, I feigned a cheerful wave. "Later," I said.

"Hey, Em," Nick called, "I don't have band practice at Watts this morning. I can give you a lift." Watts High has a jazz band Nick plays in. Our schools cooperate on several arts programs though we're rivals in just about everything else.

"It looks like a nice day. I like to walk when I can." I knew Nick just wanted the chance to pry my secret out of me. I had so much to think about and I preferred to walk this morning anyway. I didn't mind not having personal use of the car most mornings. And the exercise would cancel out the breakfast calories.

Jon and Dad, who'd veered into a debate over whether one of the ref's calls was bad or not, didn't notice me leave. I wasn't sure they'd noticed me this morning at all. Particularly considering what I suspected I might be getting myself into, that was fine with me.

As I moved through my morning at school, I felt otherworldly—almost like another person was operating my body—my real self detached, watching and waiting. I was glad when lunchtime came because that meant safe, predictable turf. Macy, Sarah, and I scored a picnic table outside. The air felt lush and warm for January so we pulled off our hoodies. I dealt Macy her chicken salad sandwich and waited for one of them to bring up something to talk about, feeling like a shaken-up soda bottle. My project revelation threatened to explode out of me at any moment, but I wasn't ready to let it.

Fortunately, the whole school was buzzing about romantic news. After more years than anyone could remember, Sam Collins and Stacy Pressley had broken up. Macy, of course, was thrilled.

"I'm actually thinking about inviting him to choir practice," she said, uncharacteristic giddiness creeping into her voice. "I might find a way to say he has a nice tone of voice. Or that I'm sorry he and Stacy broke up, but if he got lonely or bored he could come give the choir a try. Or something. What do you think?"

I blurted out, "I'm thinking of keeping my Life Skills project private. Even to friends. How about you?"

Sarah and Macy both stared at me.

"Random," Macy said. "But okey-dokey."

"How come?" Sarah asked, chasing a bite of rice mochi around her bamboo plate, using a celery stalk and a multigrain mini-muffin as utensils.

I opened my mouth to hedge the subject a little more. Out tumbled my entire project idea. I told them about the name The Motherless Child Project, and how I was inspired by the song I heard at Macy's church.

Hearing it spoken for the first time seemed bizarre. What was little more than an inspired whim now was officially out there, hanging in the space among the three of us. I braced myself. My heart felt poised to soar out of my chest with relief and encouragement from my best friends. My community project was a perfectly natural and safe idea.

"*Whoa,*" Macy said. She looked at me intently.

I waited, torn as to whether I could retract what I'd said; pass it off as a joke or something. But there was no going back. Plus, my site was registered for the project and everything. It was undoubtedly the most daring thing I'd ever done. I waited.

"That is super cool," Macy said finally and took another bite of her sandwich.

Suddenly, I felt silly acting so awkward in front of my friends. Relief flooded through me. I'd figured that, next to Dad, Macy would be my biggest obstacle. It's not that she's mean, but because she's just so frank.

I noticed Sarah was doing the sniffy-nose thing she does when she doesn't approve of something. The expression makes her look jarringly like her mother. I know Sarah tries hard to be open minded, to get out from under her mother's petty and prejudiced mindset, and I hoped she'd succeed this time. I needed her to.

"Sarah? You had something to say?" I asked, trying to sound casual. I really wanted to scream now.

"Nothing." Sarah finally speared the mochi with her celery and popped it in her mouth. Lately, Sarah chewed each bite she took for twenty seconds. It was a vegan digestion thing.

"*What?*" I pressed, hoping to mask the note of concern in my voice.

"Look, I just think it's a weird topic. I mean…" She waved her celery stick. "'Motherless child' makes it seem like there's some superhero awesome mom out there somewhere. Yours isn't…"

"Mine isn't what?" I felt my face flush, a knot beginning to form in my stomach.

"I mean, she just up and disappeared," Sarah said, dabbing her mouth with her cloth napkin. She rested her elbows on the picnic table and looked at me. "She didn't die or anything, right?" Sarah was always one of my top supporters, even over Macy sometimes. Her words stung.

"I've always wondered what happened with your mom," Macy broke in quickly, setting the last crust of her sandwich down. "It must have been something huge."

I'd known Macy since first grade and Sarah since preschool. They knew about the strange secrecy surrounding issues about my mother, but I didn't think they knew more than I did.

"I'm just looking out for you, Emily Amber," Sarah said. "I care. But Mother says any woman who gives up her children is inhuman. Maybe even dangerous." I'd always been fascinated to see how Sarah could swing from being annoyed by her mother to defending the very same points of view she said she couldn't stand. Since her mother's illness, however, she'd seemed to grow more solidly sympathetic to her mother's outlook on things.

"Well, maybe she didn't just leave," Macy retorted, her voice rising.

I felt as if I was outside my own body bobbing far above the scene now, looking down from my own bubble. My friends' voices seem to be wafting up to me as echoes. It was a feeling beyond merely lightheaded. I felt *light bodied*, if there is such a thing.

"Well, this project is about motherless children," I heard myself say. "Emphasis on *children*. It's what makes me feel different. I'm just doing what the project guidelines say to do."

Little Closer

Macy leaned over and hugged me tightly, pulling me back down to earth. I'm not generally a touchy-feely person, but I hoped she wouldn't let go, that she'd keep me tethered to the picnic table. I was either about to blow away or faint.

"You do it, girl," Macy said, giving me a reassuring squeeze. "Your topic sure beats mine."

"I just wouldn't get your hopes up about your mom," Sarah cautioned. "Only very troubled mothers lose custody of their kids."

"Lose custody?" I blinked at her, the sun smarting in my eyes. "What do you mean?"

"Will you just drop it, Sarah?" Macy hissed. "Seriously, can you hear yourself?"

Mechanically I slid out from under Macy's arm and got up from the picnic table. I swept my lunch container into my backpack and snatched my hoodie from the bench. My face burned.

Little Closer

"Emily Amber! Wait, don't go," Macy called to me, and I knew she was grabbing up her stuff, intending to follow me into the cafeteria.

"Hey, I know the song you mean!" she cried. "Is it the song that visitor girl sang in church?" She began to hum the tune.

The melody now seemed to mock me as I tried to slip out of my friend's sight, away from her perfect pitch.

5

Messages

My head was throbbing by the end of the school day. Thoughts and arguments kept bouncing around and colliding in my head. I ate the rest of my lunch between fifth and sixth periods, but the snack barely helped the emptiness in my stomach and pinching pain in my temples.

Macy found me after the final bell, as I was attempting to get down the hall and out of the school as quickly as possible. She grabbed my arm, forcing me to slow me down. "Sarah has no idea what she's talking about. Don't listen to her. She was just channeling her mom."

Messages

I stopped and looked right into Macy's eyes. They're dark and lustrous, like melting chocolate drops. "What do people know that I don't?" I demanded, right there in the hall with tons of kids also desperate to exit the premises swarming around us.

Macy shrugged and shook her head. "I honestly have no idea, Emily Amber. I've never heard anything at all about your mom, or… anything. I've only heard my mom sometimes say that it's a shame your mom isn't around, like on Mother's Day and holidays. Sarah's mom could have even made something up. Who knows with her?"

We walked outside. The temperature had dropped sharply since lunch. I stopped to fish my hoodie out of my backpack and pulled it on, tugging the hood over my head, which I rarely do. But today I wanted to hide—to be invisible. I consciously decided not to look for Nick to get a ride home. I wanted to be alone. I certainly didn't want to have my brain pried open by my brother.

Messages

"I've got Beta Club, but I'll walk with you a little ways," Macy offered.

I was glad; I did feel better having a supportive friend with me, someone who already knew what was wrong. We strode along silently for a little bit, the winter sun lightly warm on our backs.

"Uh, Macy?" I asked when we reached First Street, where she'd have to turn around and we'd have to part ways.

"Yeah?"

"About an atheist going to church and singing about God and Jesus. I wonder what Sarah's mom will say about that?"

We stared at one another for a moment. Then we burst out laughing.

Later in my room, I crouched over my laptop, hoodie still pulled over my head, with my fingers hovering over the *Delete* key. Mr. Neil had assured us in Life Skills that we could change our topics or start over for a limited time. With one stroke, I could make it all go away.

I decided to take one last good look, keep some design ideas that worked. I'd arranged some topic ideas in clickable bubbles:

Welcome! Would you like to share something about yourself? And *How do you feel about the term "motherless child?"*

Then I noticed something else. There were posts to moderate.

What? I peered closer. I counted five. The first was from Mr. Neil.

RNEIL: Great concept and design. You're very brave. Can't wait to see where this goes.

The rest were from people I didn't know:

SOULGRL: Dear Ember, I know where my mom is. But I still have 2 live without her. She & my dad got in an argument, a bad one. She fired a shot with a pistol we had, just @ the garage ceiling, not him. She just wanted 2 scare him and let neighbors know there was a problem. She pleaded self-defense. The judge ruled against her—he sentenced her 2 10 years in jail. It might turn out 2 be 5. Still, those will be all my growing up years. I miss her so bad.

MOL38: Dear Ember, ur theme song made me cry. My mother died 2 Yrs ago of Sarcomatoid renal cancer. It's a rare kidney disease. My dad and I get along good and he has a girlfriend now. I know he was lonely, and it's not like she's keeping my mother from coming back. She tries to help, to do things with me. But she's not my mom. I have a teen support group I go to after school. But I still feel lonely, like no one <u>really</u> understands. I'm glad you put up this community. I'd rather read posts than sit in a circle and talk about the same thing every week.

The third post was almost as brief as Mr. Neil's. It was by a boy with slightly mussed, dark-blond hair wearing a black Imagine Dragons T-shirt, intense blue eyes seeming to bore through a pair of rimless glasses.

His was the only avatar so far—other than mine—that was a real photo. He was cute in an angular, offbeat kind of way.

BRIGHT: Hi Ember, kewl site. People really do call me Bright, btw. My mom's been trying to get custody of me for six years. I hope she succeeds. My dad seriously blows.

Though the responses themselves were kind of shocking, I was almost as floored that anyone had found my community at all. I'd only activated *The Motherless Child Project* last night.

I remembered I had to approve all messages before they went live. I forgot all about deleting the site, I was so busy checking off the four posts I'd read: Mr. Neil's and the three new community members. Then I moved on to the last post:

LANCEB: Dear Ember, there R kids who R fatherless too. It'd be nice if we could join.

I hadn't thought about fatherless children. Heck, I hadn't really expected any *motherless* kids. I clicked the bubble to approve the message. Under it I wrote, *Hi LanceB, everyone is welcome. Glad you're here*! Then I went back and similarly greeted all the others too. To Bright, I wrote: *Hi Bright, and welcome to my community! I'm sorry you're stuck living with that kind of parent. Why won't they let you live with your mom, if that's what you and she want?*

Then, *Thanks so much, Mr. Neil.*

I sat back on my heels, still hiding under my hood, to take in the whole community page. I was both astonished and excited. Then a delicious thrill of fear rippled through me. Those post approvals I'd just made? They were final. There was no going back now. Other people were involved.

Most surprising of all? That these kids all wrote like this was normal stuff. Just like with me; my situation seemed totally weird to other people, but to me, it was my life.

The girl with her mom in jail.

Messages

The girl who was so badly missing her mom who had died.

The kid who said he was fatherless.

The boy with the strange name who was unhappy at home.

Bright.

The next morning, I poured myself a bowl of corn flakes. I used regular skim milk and sprinkled a packet of Equal on top. After yesterday, I wasn't in the mood to humor Sarah and her new vegan lifestyle. Besides, today I needed a breakfast that tasted better than cardboard and glue. Surely, Sarah could find a substitute that behaved more like real butter. I suspected the better way to go might be to find things to eat that didn't try to mimic things you *couldn't* eat.

I'd beaten everyone to the kitchen this morning as I'd hoped. As I ate, I focused on a lonely patch of glaring yellow paint on the wall just left of the stove. I'd set out to paint the whole kitchen a few years ago, aiming to

Messages

transform it from dingy beige to a cheerful Sunshine Yellow.

I found out what happens when paint dries: As you apply it, it looks just like the pleasant hue you'd chosen. Then it tends to dry to an entirely different color: Often, a color you hate.

It didn't seem like a random spot in an ugly color today, though. It occurred to me that the abandoned patch looked more like a caution sign.

"Morning, Em," Dad said.

I almost choked on my cereal.

"How's school?" he asked, browsing for a cup in the cabinet and frowning at the coffee maker, which sat cold on the counter. "You pulling up that trig grade?"

"Okay, and yes," I lied, speeding up my spoonfuls while Dad put some coffee on, then pulled up a chair beside me at the breakfast table.

"I like your new hair style," he said, looking at me. I wished I had on the hoodie. "What is that? French braid?"

"Fishtail braid," I corrected, my hand automatically flying up to my hair. "Um, thanks."

"Oh, right," he said and nodded as if he understood there was a difference. "How's that online project? Have you started it yet?"

My spoon hit the floor with a clang.

How did he...

Then I remembered. Dad had to sign my permission slip a week ago for me to hand in to Mr. Neil. *Note to self: Ask Mr. Neil if parents have to approve the choice of community sites.*

O.M.G.

"Not really," I hedged. "I'm still working on my topic." My heart was thumping in my chest. I jumped up to pick up the fallen spoon, and threw it in the sink. Once again I had the distinct feeling I was doing something wrong, without quite knowing why.

"Jon, where's that training release form?" Dad called in the direction of the stairs. "I don't know why I need to keep signing these. You're nineteen years old.

Guess I'm the one with the insurance. But I need to get going in a minute."

While Dad signed Jon's form, I snatched my cereal bowl off the table and poured what was left of the corn flakes down the disposal. I hoped the loud grating of the disposal gears was drowning out the racket I imagined my heart was making.

I grabbed a Lunchable Lean from the fridge, snatched up my backpack and hoodie and slipped out the kitchen door.

Sarah rushed up to me the second she saw me round the corner onto First Street. She knew the days Nick had jazz band and couldn't drive me. She must have made quite a case to her mother, who usually drives her to school at the last minute. She doesn't want Sarah hanging with "loiterers and potheads" before school. Mrs. Goddard does kind of have a point though. Our school might have a large population of privileged kids, but in most ways it's the same as other schools. Our "loiterers" just hang out in the parking lot behind more expensive cars.

Sarah's stuck-up, sniffy expression from yesterday seemed to have melted back to normal.

"I didn't mean to hurt your feelings, Emily Amber. I'm sorry." She grabbed my right hand in her two and squeezed tight. The sharp bezel of her mood ring cut right into my finger.

"Ow!" I cried, reflexively slipping my hand into my hoodie pocket. I noticed the crystal in her ring was a dull orangey-yellow. If dark blue meant bliss, Sarah must be miserable, I thought.

"Oops! I'm so sorry, Emily Amber," Sarah said, looking positively wretched at this point.

To be honest, with all the commotion in my head, I'd just about forgotten her negative reaction when I'd described my project at lunch the day before.

"Well, I don't want to get too deep into this project," I said offhandedly. I didn't want to go into it with Sarah this morning, when I was already beginning

Messages

to seriously worry. In fact, I was burning to get to Mr. Neil before class so I could talk to him about the privacy possibilities for the assignment. "I want to meet more people like me. I mean that's the assignment, right? Might as well make the most of it."

"I understand completely," Sarah said, her voice perking up. "I've never really thought about life without a mom, except when I wish my mom would take a really long trip." She looked so earnest, I had to suppress a giggle.

We'd been friends for so long, I was sure Sarah must have spilled her mom's opinion of my home situation sometime back in the day, but I couldn't remember. You know how you learn to shut out things that you can't do anything about? Skate over them?

"Um, have you chosen another community to join?" Sarah asked as we walked along. What good would it do to not forgive that slip, even if it was a painful one? Plus, I needed all the friends and support I could get, because I suspected life at home was about to get real tricky.

I shook my head. "Been too busy. You?"

"I was thinking about joining a quilting community," Sarah said. "There are two that I've seen. People think quilting is this pioneer, old-lady thing. And I've been wanting to try to learn something beyond knitting. They say these kinds of crafts are like yoga for your brain." She tapped her temple with her forefinger.

Sarah and her mother are serious yarn wizards. They can knit or crochet anything—slippers and mitts to dolls and doilies.

I'd vaguely thought about looking for a teen yoga community to join, but didn't think I'd find one since yoga is hardly unusual. I didn't think anyone would feel "different" for practicing yoga but, I didn't know anyone who quilted.

"Hey, why don't we both join the same quilting group?" I suggested. I had no idea how I would fit learning to quilt into my increasingly troubling and emotional schedule, but I'd meant to learn to sew one of these days. This might be an excellent way to start.

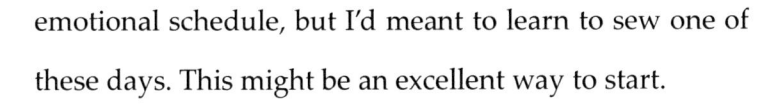

Heaven knows I needed outlets.

6

Bright

"Well," Mr. Neil said when I skipped my mid-morning primping session in the girls' restroom in order to pepper him with community questions before class. "I can't promise complete secrecy from your father on this—you're a minor in the home—but I understand your concern."

He reassured me the privacy settings were such that no one who was not a part of the project could access the communities unless the user chose to share. "We're walking a rather thin line here, but we're prepared for thin lines. We'll have a backup from Guidance if we run into situations that might require...

extra support. Kids have so much to deal with these days. I've already flagged a couple that might need a little assistance.

"Personally, I like your project topic a lot. I firmly believe every child, no matter what age, should have the right to explore his or her own feelings about a missing parent. It's getting rough out there in the divorce and custody world. Kids are too often caught in the middle of a war they don't belong in. Many don't have anywhere to go where they can meet other kids in their same boat."

Divorce and custody stuff was over my head and I didn't know how it would apply to me at all, no matter what bunk Sarah was spouting off yesterday. "Yeah, and one girl's mom *died,*" I added, throwing my hands up for emphasis. "She said she was so glad someone started a community like this." I felt guilty using this poor girl's—*MOL38's*—situation to prop up my resolve but it made me feel better anyway.

Mr. Neil added, "I'll do what I can to help you run interference if your dad wants to know more about the project, to explain what we're trying to accomplish with it. It's my feeling you should discuss it with him yourself. Has he already signed the permission slip?"

I nodded, knowing full well I hadn't chosen my topic when I got Dad to sign—a knowledge that was only beginning to tug at my conscience. I was tempted to ask Mr. Neil if community topics had to be approved when the parents signed, but I just let the moment hang. I needed a loophole.

A mere two days ago, I'd have used this conversation with Mr. Neil to switch my topic to something safer, something like Help I Have a Fashion Addiction! I often wonder now if I could have changed the course of things if I'd chickened out or if the truth would have just tracked me down from behind and pounced at another time.

But right now, I knew I had to keep the Motherless Child Project going and that I had to keep it a secret from my dad. How could I not, really? I had these kids trusting and depending on me now. I'd already designed everything and I wanted information for myself too. And, there was this potentially fascinating guy there. Not necessarily in that order.

"Thanks so much, Mr. Neil. This helps a lot," I said, reflexively glancing at his left hand. The naked white band of skin remained, still remembering the ring. Perhaps my topic was hitting home for him too.

I'd already decided to spend lunch in the school library. I told Macy and Sarah to go on without me since I needed to look up something. I said I would meet them toward the end of lunch if I could. Personal laptops weren't allowed at our school, just the standard-issue keyboards and iPads restricted to note taking.

"Strange," Macy said, referring to my usual attitude about the library. "But okey-dokey." It wasn't the books or the artificial quiet about the place that got to me. It was the décor. Or lack of it I guess. I found the gaping, colorless space profoundly depressing and I avoided it as much as possible.

Bright

I didn't say so—mainly because Sarah was standing there—but pumped after talking with Mr. Neil, I was dying to see if there was any more activity on my community. I now felt a sort of pride in having created a place other kids wanted to be. This combination of curiosity and ego fueled my courage to do this behind Dad's back. It was like an invisible but strong cord drawing me forward.

The library was dull and silent as a graveyard, a tomb of dead books. I've never been in a tomb but the library smelled like I thought one would, like ancient dirt mixed with the dust of rotten leaves and heaven knows what else. I found a free computer and lugged up one of the chunky oak chairs, whose "wear-and-tear resistant" quality always seemed to me to be kind of pathetically hopeful. They looked as new as they probably had the day somebody first hauled them into the library.

I dug into my backpack for my iPhone, making sure it was on airplane mode and unplugged my earbuds. I hoped they would sync up on this computer. I'd obviously never tried and I didn't want to have to mute the volume. My *Motherless Child* soundtrack was becoming as important to me as the community.

"*Sometimes I feel like a motherless child…*" This was the clear, young but strong voice of a high school singer named Grace Bobber. Hers was my favorite version, maybe even more than that guest singer Chloe, the one I'd heard at Cross Path that first time. Every now and then, I searched YouTube for more versions to add. I meant to message Grace sometime to see if maybe she had a CD.

There were two new members and seven new comments on my community. For a moment, I just stared transfixed at the gently buzzing screen. My site seemed massive and more important somehow on the larger library screen than it did on my compact laptop. It seemed *real* and not just something I slapped together in my own room.

Bright

I needed to stick to business since lunch was only thirty-five minutes. Plus, now I'd have to approve topic threads too. And, I would have to review them first of course.

Lance B., the boy who'd asked about fatherless children, had posted some of his story.

LANCEB: I've never known my dad. I only know there was a wicked court battle when I was a baby. I guess he lost. My mom won't let anybody talk about him. I don't even know if they were married and I don't know anybody from his family. It's like they don't exist at all. But I know they do and this is what bothers me most about the whole thing. I've just never known what to do about it. Maybe I'll find some answers here.

I noticed he'd chosen Captain America as his avatar. I wondered if it referred to him or maybe the dad he didn't know.

Then another newcomer:

Bright

QUEENOFPINK: I'm soooo glad I found U Ember. My mom stopped coming to see us when I was 6. Now and then, me and my sister try to find her but she never gets back to us. We've always wondered if we did something wrong. I guess we must have but we're trying to fix whatever. It's so sad...

As I read through the posts, automatically approving each one, an instant message appeared on my screen.

BRIGHT: Hey Ember.

My heart lurched. This boy was definitely growing on me, with his messy hair and his incredibly white teeth.

I had no idea if IM's were allowed on this project. I'd need to ask Mr. Neil tomorrow morning. But if Bright could activate it, I guessed it was OK at least for now.

Hey, I wrote, nerves tingling in my fingers.

BRIGHT: Hot topic.
ME: Sure looks like it!

Bright

While I waited in a state of suspended excitement to see if he'd send something back, I scanned the rest of the community to make sure everything looked okay. Some kids had struck up conversations with others on the message board and added a few new topics. One was: *What can we do about this?* I'd have to wait until later to read the comments sprinkled under the thread.

Bloop. Incoming.

BRIGHT: U getting any flack about ur project?
ME: No. Why?
BRIGHT: That's good. This needs 2 happen.

What needs to happen? I thought, but before I could message back, the bell rang. It seemed only seconds since I'd sat down.

ME: Gotta go, lunch over. Talk l8er?
BRIGHT: Kewl
ME: Um, are you feeling any better about your—situation?

Bright

BRIGHT: Nope. Never changes. Don't worry about me. TTYL.

This project was making me bold. I'd never messaged something overtly personal to a guy so soon—especially not a cute one like Bright. Macy says I play hard to get but I don't think that's really so. Maybe since I have brothers around, I don't view boys as the exotic creatures my friends do. It takes a lot to impress me.

I wrote a general message before signing off:

ME: Thanks all of you for sharing your stories. I might not have any answers for you myself, but maybe as we learn about each other's situations we can come up with ideas.

"Look at you, held up in the *library*," Macy teased in mock admiration as I arrived only a split-second before the bell for P.E.—still tugging my gym sweats over my jeans and T-shirt. I had two tardies already, both from primping and talking too long in the girls' room. A third would get me a demerit and that would get me study hall during lunch. I needed my lunchtime now more than ever.

Bright

"I can't believe how busy your site is already," Macy said when I breathlessly reported my newest activity.

Coach Manigault was queuing us up for layups, which I hate because I kind of suck at sports. Worse, my stomach was growling and I was beginning to feel floaty. If I was going to keep blowing off lunch, I'd have to sneak at least a few bites of Lunchable Lean at my locker or bring Luna bars or something. It occurred to me that this was one of the few times I'd unconsciously skipped a meal. I mean, I did it all the time, but it was deliberate. I felt proud of myself in a totally twisted way.

"Last time I checked, I only had two members in my community," Macy sighed as we inched forward in our line. "And one is on the fence about being an atheist."

I didn't want to hurt her feelings by telling her there was even more activity on mine now. Instead, I said, "I had no idea so many people live without a mom. Dads too. It's kind of crazy." I was tempted to tell her

Bright

about Bright, because I was dying to by now, but Casey Johnson threw Macy the basketball and she was gone.

Nick texted to offer me a ride home after school. He's like a Schnauzer. He can always tell when I'm holding something in and he'll pester me until I drop it. By this time, I didn't mind so much. I felt I had to tell someone in my family about my project in case something happened with it somehow. I had Mr. Neil at school but I needed an ally on the homefront. It would naturally be Nick.

I didn't think I could stand feeling like I was about to explode into a bundle of nerves at home anyway.

I just had to find the right time.

7

Threshold

When I got home and to my room, I immediately logged on to my community. There were only a handful of new posts since lunchtime. But, I figured most kids were still at school or activities after. Bright had more formally messaged the Welcome thread.

BRIGHT: My full name is David Brightman Benson. My mom always called me "Bright." I had totally white hair when I was little and you can probably see I have really blue eyes. I guess the name stuck.

A couple of girls had posted cutesy responses to Bright's post. Already, he was causing a stir. And for some reason this rankled me. This was *my* community. I know—immaturity central—but I promised to tell the whole truth here. And, the truth is what I'm about now or trying to be anyway.

I plunked out an IM to Bright. I hadn't gotten around to asking Mr. Neil about IM protocol, but right now, I didn't care.

ME: Ember's a nickname, too. My real name is Emily Amber. Why can't u just go live with your mom if you don't like being with your dad?
...
ME: If u don't mind me asking.
BRIGHT: It's kewl. I want people to know. A quick answer to your question is the judge won't let me.
ME: Judge? Aren't U allowed to choose what parent U want to be with when you're like 14?
BRIGHT: Not everywhere. Not when there's blatant disregard for the rules or the kids. They can make you do whatever they want or try to.

ME: Who's they?

BRIGHT: Long story. I'll tell you sometime. Meantime, you can check out my YouTube videos if you want. I post at least once a week.

ME: OK What do I look under?

BRIGHT: Just look under Bright Benson.

ME: U use your real name?

ME: I mean that's really bold. U can post them here on the community too if U want.

…..

…..

BRIGHT: Well, I want people to know who I am 4 practical reasons but I don't want to get you in trouble.

ME: Trouble?

A chill shot up my spine. I wasn't sure it was the good kind of chill either.

BRIGHT: Just causing stink about custody crap. Saying they shouldn't stick me with my dad. I don't mean trouble to regular people—just with the powers that be.

Threshold

I was wondering who the "powers that be" were when Dad's voice boomed up the stairs.

"Emily Amber! Nick! Dinner!"

ME: Gotta go down for dinner. Dad's cook night. If I survive, I'll look up ur videos later.

....

ME: Thanks for sharing them!

BRIGHT: Kewl. At least your dad cooks Good luck

For the record, Dad actually *can* cook. I know there are lots of great male chefs and all. I love Gordon Ramsay and all the food and cooking network people. For someone who tries to eat as little as possible, I'm kind of obsessed with food. After I got my license, Dad started sending me to the Piggly Wiggly with a list and his credit card. It's kind of a mixed blessing, but at least I can pick out the healthier versions of stuff, like brown rice instead of white, even though everybody complains.

That "survival" bit I said to Bright was just to sound cool, like I was commiserating about having a bad dad. I felt a jab of guilt; I didn't necessarily think Dad was a bad parent. He was just Dad. Dad with a temper. Dad, who used to throw stuff and slam doors when he drank a lot (which he didn't so much anymore). Dad, whose voice, when angry, used to rattle the teeth in my head. Dad, who, for all his church involvement, seemed to think women aren't as good as men.

Then there was Dad who carefully shopped for that car for Nick and me, reading all the Consumer Reports and opting for the old Volvo because it had the highest safety rating and he knew the car lot owner, so we wouldn't be driving a lemon. Dad who always volunteered at my school on Community Day when I was little. Dad who made me so proud when he showed his careful engineering drawings and what they eventually would turn into. Dad who at every school or church play or ball game, clapped and yelled the loudest of anyone in the audience or the stands.

Threshold

I made a mental note to correct my wisecrack about Dad's cooking next time I IM'd Bright. To say what a good meal Dad had made. Or something.

I was also starving, and glad it was Dad's cook night because he always makes dinner early. It was Wednesday, so he had Promise Keepers at the church. Jon was at work and then probably had a training session as usual. Ashley had been buried in her classes. We didn't see much of either of them lately. Sometimes I actually kind of missed Ashley, to tell you the truth.

Dad had made one of his standbys, shrimp and rice with Faith Foods freezer rolls that plump up in the oven. I'd started buying the multigrain, which made me feel better about devouring them nearly whole like I always end up doing.

"Okay you guys, I'm out," Dad said, rising from the table and dropping his dinner plate and glass in the sink. "Take care of the dishes, please?" he said to me.

"All right." Then I surprised myself by going over to Dad and hugging him tight around his waist. He winced a little. I guess it was unusual. Like I said, I've never been a hugger so I'm not sure what made me do it.

But I stood there clinging to him like a four-year-old who doesn't want a parent to leave. I felt my project weighing heavy on my shoulders. It seemed to have become part of my person. I'd known from the moment I created the community that it had the distinct possibility of getting me in major trouble with Dad. Mentioning our mom had always been grounds for major retribution, so that the subject was all but dead.

But for the first time I wondered if basing my project around this same mom was a betrayal of my dad somehow?

Confused and embarrassed, I broke from Dad and pretended to mess with my hair, producing a hairband from my jeans pocket and looping it into a knot on my head.

"Just do your homework and get to bed at a decent hour," he said. "Son?" Dad opened the kitchen door and called to Nick through the garage, where he'd slipped out probably to grab his amp. "Don't be too late if you practice at the Scheins'. You know I'm not real fond of the way they let those kids have the run of the place."

"Bye Dad," I said.

I peeked out the door a few minutes after Dad's Beamer pulled out of the driveway. Nick was putting his amp in the back of the Volvo. He practices with his alt-rock band, the Wingnuts, at least two nights a week and sometimes more if they have a gig coming up. They're still figuring out their sound—that's what they say anyway—but people turn out. It helps that the Scheins are among the most loved people in town.

"I've gotta get my guitar and stuff from my room. Wanna come up?"

On the way to Nick's room, I grabbed my laptop from my bed where I'd left it. *Note to self: You're committing to follow through on this so you better find a safer place to keep it.*

Threshold

I waited for Nick to fish the key to his room out of his jeans pocket. He'd put a padlock on the door years ago. I suspected it was because of my snooping even though I'd long outgrown it.

"Pew, it smells like a head shop in here," I said, pinching the bridge of my nose.

"Oops, I left the incense burning during supper." Nick went over to his bureau and picked up the smoldering skeleton of an incense stick. "Hey, how do you know what a head shop smells like?"

"You could burn down the house doing that," I said, ignoring his question as I sat down on the twin bed nearest the door. I opened my laptop to locate my site. I might as well show him now. Plus, whatever the fallout might be, it would be short and sweet since he was leaving.

Nick hoisted up the window beside his bureau. A cool brace of air swept in.

"What's with the Daddy's girl thing?"

Threshold

By the time Nick turned around from brushing the sooty trail of incense ash on his dresser with a sock, I was snapping shut the laptop and moving toward the door.

"Hey, Em!" As I reached for the doorknob, Nick grabbed me gently by my shoulder. "What's wrong? Hey, sorry about the Daddy's girl crack. It was just different to see you acting that way. I didn't mean anything by it."

For a few beats I stood staring at the closed door, Nick waiting behind me. Patchouli. Definitely patchouli. Was he bathing in it?

Finally, I turned around. "Okay. But no jokes and no laughing at me or making me feel stupid."

Nick went over and sat in the one chair in the room, a ladder back he sits in to play his guitar. "I never try to make you look stupid, Ember. You always do fine with that all by yourself."

I shot him my warning look. Nick grinned. "Just kidding. Anyway, promise. What's going on?"

Threshold

Then it all overflowed—the project and my community and Sarah's mother's opinion of a mother who's not in the picture. I noticed Nick's lips tighten. I told him about all the kids without their mothers who'd joined my community and the one—Lance B.—who was with his mother and didn't want to be.

For a few moments, Nick just sat looking at me and it wasn't his "okay, what's up?" expression. It was the "I'm mulling over something incredibly profound and I must carefully decide whether or not it is over your head" look.

Instead of uttering something completely inaccessible, he said, "Can I have a look? At your... site?"

I got up and set the computer firmly in his lap, backing away as if entrusting a fussy baby to someone I wasn't sure about, but glad to get rid of it for a few minutes.

Nick surveyed my community, clicking here and there and occasionally making a face or shaking his head.

"Flamer," he muttered. "You get many of those?"

"Many what?" I asked, leaning over his shoulder in spite of myself. I read Lance B.'s latest post: *STOP GLAMORIZING MOTHERS, YOU MORONS!!*

Lance B. seemed to be getting angrier and nastier every day.

Nick went back to scrolling. I was beginning to actually feel proud for him to see all the posts, even if Lance B.'s were of the insulting variety. At least in terms of the assignment, it was a definite success.

There were a couple of new threads too—*Nowhere to Turn* and *Some Vids from Bright*.

"Bright? Is that a person?"

"Uh, yeah," I said, "it's a nickname." Nick's brow furrowed as he read.

Then I just couldn't wait anymore and asked him flat-out: "What do you think? I mean, of me doing a project on this? Even though we're not allowed to bring it up around here, it doesn't mean something isn't there.

I'm confused… and in the dark… .and I don't even know why."

Nick, his face in full frown now, glanced at his Fossil Swiss watch, which is his most precious possession next to his guitar. "Sheesh, it's already 7:30. Ember, I've got to go so we don't practice too late again. Now is a superb time to not tick Dad off."

"But do you think what I'm doing with my project is okay?" I pressed, already feeling nervous about being alone in the house without at least support from one person.

But I noticed Nick was smiling a little as he snapped his guitar case shut, carefully tucking in the hand-tooled Wingnuts guitar strap the Scheins had gotten the band members during Hanukkah last year. "Looks like something you'd get at a Six Flags souvenir shop," Dad had said when Nick slung it over his shoulder, running his fingers over the perfectly honed letters.

Threshold

"Em, there are about a million things I could say right now," Nick said in a measured tone. "But for now I guess I'll just say I'm glad. Yeah, I'm glad you're doing this. You can't believe how glad I am. Now I see why you were trying to get on Dad's good side after dinner tonight."

Well, that hadn't been it. That hadn't been it at all. But it felt good to smile.

8

BostonBaked

We've known the Scheins for as long as I can remember. Mr. Schein and Dad work for the same company, ChemSouth, which relocated both of them from Atlanta eons ago when they merged with ChemBay in Charleston. Actually, I was born at Piedmont Hospital in Buckhead, which is Atlanta's nicest neighborhood, or at least it was then. Mrs. Schein, who worked there back in the day, requested she be the assisting nurse on the day I was born. I kind of just love that story. Mrs. Schein tells it to me at least once a year at one of their annual parties: Fourth of July, Halloween, and so on.

BostonBaked

I was a couple of weeks early, a breech baby, which means that my feet were where my head should have been. Apparently, it was quite the drama for a while. The doctor was preparing for a C-section, but I managed to reposition myself. It was as if I was somehow suddenly aware I was going the wrong way and turned around. No one seems to know or at least remember all that except for Mrs. Schein. It's nice to have someone know you from the moment you appeared in this world.

Anyway, you'd think those two would be friends, Dad and Mr. Schein, but they're not. To hear Dad talk, it's because he thinks Mr. Schein is too liberal with his kids. Dad doesn't think friends should be allowed to hang out all the time at all hours. And, Dad doesn't like that Mr. Schein permits his sons Scotty and Adam to have an occasional beer. I don't see what's so wrong with that. The Schein boys are known for being really smart and polite—not drunken idiots. But I could tell it went deeper than parenting with my Dad.

"I'm David Brightman Benson, aka Bright," said the now unbearably cute boy in the video. I was struck by several things in watching him live. His eyes seemed to pierce through the camera lens like he could see you. He had a graceful way of using his hands, even though the tips of his fingernails were raw and red. And, there was the awfulness of his story.

"Maybe you're visiting my channel for the first time. Maybe you've seen the dozens of other videos I've posted over the past three and a half years documenting the abuse I'm forced to live with. And, worse, it's at the hands of this man who everyone thinks is the… freaking most successful, socially upstanding man they ever met.

"I would really like to be able to sit here and say that telling the truth about that so-called great man—my father Peter Benson—has made a difference.

"Well, you know what's changed since I started telling the truth? A very long six and a half years ago?

"Nothing. That's what's changed.

"You know those posters, commercials and radio spots telling kids they need to tell someone if they're being abused?

"Well, I've lost count of the times I told—even begged—people trying to get help. I called Child Protective Services myself. When people described my situation to the police, any investigation that followed was a joke.

"The family court judge does nothing. They won't let me speak in court. They won't hear any evidence my mom and I collect. There's mountains of it. The lawyer—the Guardian ad Litem who's supposed to act in my best interests—the one who just conveniently happens to be my new stepmother? Well, she also does nothing.

"That great institution, a place where you're supposed to find justice, just returns me to the abusive home.

"So, the testimony of the abused goes utterly ignored. Why does everyone always believe the abuser?

They go on appearance—my dad seems like such a great guy—and they ignore solid documentation to the contrary.

"Over the years, the police have done two things: they've hauled me back 'home' after I tried to escape the abuse on my own and they treated the abuser himself, Peter Benson, as the pillar of society. They treated me like a runaway, a no-good piece of trash who left a perfect home.

"Needless to say, they refuse to press charges against him.

"So, I'm seventeen now. I can be emancipated, right? I'm over sixteen. I can just go live with my mom or go be on my own, right? But it doesn't work that way in the world I and countless others live in, especially if you speak up about abuse.

"That's how my mom lost custody in the first place. She reported the abuse. She told the truth. The result? They took me away from her and put me solely in the hands of my abuser.

"So, I'm asking you now—not just for me—but for all the kids who are forced to live with their abusers, to please listen. Please do all you can to get the powers that be to see beyond that polished image the abuser maintains and see the truth.

"It might be too late for me. But, I'm never gonna quit trying. I'm not just looking to help myself, but to help others who are forced to live the way I do.

"Peace out."

Bloop. IM incoming.

BRIGHT: u survive dinner?

My heart did a backflip.

ME: LOL, yes

...

ME: My dad is a really great cook, so I was just joking. I mean, he's not a bad dad. He's just...
BRIGHT: That's kewl.
ME: Watching your videos. It's... they're... scary and terrible.

BRIGHT: *Yeah, it sucks bigtime.*

ME: *U don't worry they'll.... Uh, whoever, will... get U in more trouble?*

BRIGHT: *I'm all over the Internet anyway. I can't get help if I don't. TV guys do stories about me and my mom posts for help too. I'm famous for being in a situation that no one can or will help me get out of.*

ME: *I don't get why U can't see ur mom? Who can stop U?*

BRIGHT: *Not allowed to see or even talk to her on the phone.*

ME: *How*

ME: *I mean, why? I'm soooo confused.*

BRIGHT: *The more u get into this, the more you'll see and understand it. Courts are corrupt. There's money from the government—lots of it—meant to help families and specifically violent households. Except people use the money to exploit the system. It's all about the money. The parents get used too.*

ME: *I still don't get why? Why would people do this to the kids and the moms?*

BRIGHT: Encourage fathers to fight child support. Control. Abusive men want to punish the mother for leaving. Have complete access to the kid. Break them all. Any and all of the above I guess.

BRIGHT: There's a lot out there about it, articles and info, for the mothers and even the kids. But, the advocates and the lawyers for the dads steamroll it all. Ur smart. You'll start to get it. I know it sounds cray right now.

Well, that was true. I didn't get it at all. I had to think to drum up something to even say next.

ME: Your stepmother—why is she allowed to handle ur case? That seems kind of unfair.

BRIGHT: Welcome to my world.

Other posts were beginning to pile up, but I felt I needed to end the conversation on a positive note.

ME: Ur doing this through school, right? Have U started your own community?

BRIGHT: Yeah, haven't gotten a good start yet. Unlike u. :>0

ME: *LOL, what's your topic?*

ME (to myself): *Please don't let it be Dungeons and Dragons. Or Magic: The Gathering. Or Wicca. Or comic books of any kind... Or, oh please no Star Wars or Star Trek...*

BRIGHT: *My topic is languages. I speak five languages and I'm learning Japanese now. I guess you could say I collect languages. Know another language collector?*

I laughed aloud. *Oh, thank you, God. I really mean that.*

ME: *No, but this is very cool! Which ones?*

BRIGHT: *Well, English obviously and Spanish, German, Italian, Swahili...*

ME: *Swahili?*

BRIGHT: *Well, I start veering off when I leave and do homeschool.*

ME: *When U leave?*

BRIGHT: *Yes. Like I say in my videos, I've done it twice, left I mean, but they've hauled me back here. They won't next time.*

BoStonBaked

ME (running out of things to say and desperately needing time to process all this information): *Well, guess I'd better go approve some posts.*

BRIGHT: *Ur site is getting busy. It's great what ur doing.*

ME: *Hey, in case U ever want to talk outside of here about what's going on at home, my cell is 803-555-1250.*

BRIGHT: *Thx. I'll probably not be on here by the time project is over. If I leave, I'll be leaving school too.*

ME: *I wish I could help.*

BRIGHT: *You're helping already by doing this. Asante sana. Tuonane baadaye.*

BRIGHT: *That's Swahili for thank you very much. Good night!*

ME: *Good night. Bright.*

BRIGHT: *Hey, you log off first.*

ME: *No you.*

BRIGHT: *I'm making u log off only so u can finish whatever you've got to do, homework or whatever. Not because I want to.*

BRIGHT: *Someone so beautiful has got to be busy.*

I flushed deep pink, and I didn't care because I was in my room alone, and it felt heavenly.

[BRIGHT logged off]

JOY1989: Can someone please help my mom or let us know who could maybe help in Ohio. We're near Columbus. Here's what happened. My mom went to all this trouble to get a fair mental exam from this psychologist she hired on her own because the one the court made her use for the custody trial was packed full of lies. There were so many lies, she didn't even recognize it was about her!

Anyway, she spent so much money for this new exam and all. Then, when she went to the judge to present it, she wouldn't accept the new psychologist's exam!! She started shouting I guess to try to get the judge to listen to her, and the judge had the "guards"—whoever they are—arrest her!! This was all because she was frustrated that the judge wouldn't listen to her. Why would they arrest her for trying to get them to hear the truth?? Anyway, this was Friday and it's already Tuesday!! I don't know how to get her out of jail. I don't have any money and even my mom's family seems to side with my dad. There is no one I can call. I'm so worried. So upset.

A post by an unfamiliar name, with no avatar, appeared.

BOSTONBAKED: You children are falling prey to a very unfortunate trend here. There is a minor—very fringe—movement that is trying to convince parents and kids alike that the Family Court system is unjust. This is altogether untrue. Joy1989—bless you. I know you think your mother did the right thing, but she obviously made a big mistake and is paying dearly for it. She was in contempt of court. She should have been advised better. This is why the judge rightfully had her arrested. It's high time the judges began trusting the evidence their own experts give them and not letting them be manipulated by crocodile tears from hysterical mothers who just want their own way. It is true Fathers are being granted custody more often and Fathers as Parents have assumed their rightful place at the forefront. But, it's because some equality was needed. If the government sees fit to award custody to deserving Fathers, both in court and through federal funding that assists them in getting the proper support, who are you to question it? Are you saying that a court of law, a sound and wise judge and very capable agents of the court are not qualified to do their jobs?

Why not seriously challenge these women—forgive me, but those like your mom—who complain that the system is somehow working against them? They complain about the psychological exams they failed and the testimony against them, and say their attorneys didn't work on their behalf and didn't want to help the children. They say nobody bothered to find out what's really behind their loss of custody. If you truly want to understand what is really happening, visit father-ledfamilies.us. Good luck to you. I would look to your Father for guidance from now on. Your mother's parents would not have taken your Father's side for no reason. This is a hard lesson I know, but it's time for you to respect the judge's decision and move on with your life.

When I tried to find out who BostonBaked was, I got a blank entry even though all the kids in the project were required to use the logins and other non-personal information the schools gave us. The rule was if a parent monitored the project, he or she had to use the same login info as the students.

And this most certainly wasn't the post of a kid. For one thing, he called us "children." For another, he seemed to be speaking a different language. *Cue Bright? Do you speak BostonBaked?* I had no idea what BostonBaked was talking about, only that he seemed to be saying the courts were fair while Bright and the other kids were wrong.

I supposed BostonBaked could be a kid's parent. But whose? Not LanceB., since he said he'd never known his dad. Although, BostonBaked sounded just like a grownup version of him.

Because I didn't know what else to do at the moment, I approved the post.

GRETAGURL: Mr. Baked, ur scary but people like you are the reason my mother is in the hospital. She had a breakdown after the custody hearing and the judge she got was really mean and messed up. It wasn't her fault. Go away.

SOULGRRL: BostonBaked, you don't know anything about my personal situation or my mother's or Ember's or anyone else's. You don't even have a profile, so we know you're a troll just hiding out.

BOSTONBAKED: I know more than you'd ever think possible. And I'm willing to bet the mother of any child on this board who lost custody had a million strikes against her. Truth is, they have every defense and Fathers have been on the wrong end of the court's decisions for too long. What makes you think your mothers were justified in arguing with the court's decision? I'm sorry you kids have been brainwashed to think that somehow "the system" has failed them and you.

QUEENOFPINK: ??? Who are you? What right do you have to come here and tell us that what we see with our own eyes isn't true? Well, I know the truth and so do the rest of us here. We don't need liars like you coming on here and blasting us from reporting what we see nearly every day. My mother loves me! I might not be able to see her, but I know it in my heart.

BOSTONBAKED: So if I understand you correctly, you're saying that the entire legal system and the concerned Dads out there just trying to protect ourselves and our children from further harm are against you? I'm really sorry you have to live this way. Maybe if your Father had custody, you'd have somewhere else to go other than this pathetic forum.

QUEENOFPINK: My father does have custody! Why are you calling Ember's forum pathetic? This is for school! We love Ember!! We love the Motherless Child Project! It gives us a place to go and talk about things.

BOSTONBAKED: To trade half-baked lies is more like it.

Then there were about ten posts supporting QueenofPink and saying what an excellent job I'd done on the forum, how glad they were to meet others like them and how much they were learning. One said she'd found the first real new friend she'd made in years, SoulGrrl, and even if they hadn't met in person yet that they planned to try to get together over the summer.

While I sat with my fingers twitching over the keyboard, trying to decide what to do, a couple of other posts surfaced:

BOSTONBAKED: Okay kids, play nice and go do your homework. In other words, get a life. You're accomplishing nothing here.

JEREMY21: I hope Ember doesn't mind if I step in on her behalf on this convo, but I'd advise everyone to not respond to BostonBaked. Either someone is trying to get our goats—that's what my grandma used to say—or he's going to make serious trouble. Ember, I think you need to report this to your Life Skills teacher.

Feeling grateful to be told what to do without quite having to make the decision myself, I sent an IM to Mr. Neil.

ME: Mr. Neil, there is this guy who's crashed my community. He's BostonBaked. Can U take a look at this conversation? It's

9:15 p.m. Thurs. He's upsetting a bunch of kids. I approved his posts so far. Don't know what to do. Thanks, Emily Amber

Out of total nowhere, a snippet of scripture elbowed its way into my mind. Scripture and memorized bits do that to me sometimes. This was a verse we'd learned for Vacation Bible School at my cousin Jilly's little country church when I was visiting one summer: *Be watchful. Your adversary, the devil, walks around like a roaring lion, seeking whom he may devour. 1 Peter 5.*

We don't talk so much about the devil around here. Even the Lord's Prayer neatly sidesteps Satan by asking *the Lord* not to lead us to temptation, but deliver us from evil. Charlestonians are like that. Jilly's church? Totally all about taking it up directly with Satan. *Get behind me, Satan!* we chanted in our summer seersucker shorts and Vacation Bible School T-shirts from the slick sanctuary pews. *You are a stumbling block to me; you do not have in mind the concerns of God, but merely human concerns. Matthew 16:23.*

I'm not saying this guy was the devil cause how would I know? It's just what popped into my mind. Maybe, he was like what they call a "devil's advocate." Whatever he was, he was going to wreck my community. I hoped Mr. Neil would at least tell me I could block people.

BostonBaked hadn't logged in legitimately and that ought to be enough.

By the time I finally checked my cell phone, which I'd had on Airplane mode all this time, it was throbbing with messages.

MACY: Call me! (x 6)

SARAH: Want to come over tomorrow and we can get started quilting? Mother is setting up the sewing machine for us to use. Here's a link to the community I found for us to join.

Sounds good, I texted back. *I'll check out the link. Thx.* It would be a huge relief to do something fun and creative and I hadn't spent one on one time with Sarah in forever.

UNKNOWN NUMBER: *Hi Ember, it's Bright. Snapchatting this. Will destruct right after u open. Makes me feel like James Bond. I'll be ditching this phone soon, but I wanted to say hi.*
ME: *Hey!*
BRIGHT: *Well, you have a good night's rest, okay beautiful? You deserve it.*
ME: *So do you.*
BRIGHT: *It feels great to hear that! Talk live tomorrow maybe?*

    Oh yeah.

9

Threads

I made a cup of Sleepytime Tea and Skyped Macy. As soon as I saw her brown eyes bleary and bulgy like they get when she's been staring at the computer screen too long, I knew I wasn't going to have to say anything. She clearly wanted to talk about problems in her own world. Obviously, it was her community because her Life Skills textbook and notes were splayed on her bedspread and intermingled with apparently every hair weave she owned. The hanks in her hair were electric lime and a shocking blue, and they were skewed at angles even more unnatural than their colors. She looked like an exotic bird coming out of a bad fight.

"Well," she said, "I have ten kids in my community now. They're cool and all, but being an atheist seems so... well, *final*. It seems like once you decide on it, there's no going back. I'm not sure I'm really ready for that kind of commitment."

I'd always privately thought Macy's conversion to atheism had been a snap decision. After all, she'd made it following an argument with her parents. They wanted her to go to Catechism class, which was required to become a church member. And she wanted no part of it.

She'd sung in the choir for years, hadn't she? Macy reasoned. Now they wanted to make her hand over ten percent of her allowance for the tithe? And then there was the fact that Catechism was held on Wednesdays after school and the Beta Club happened to meet at the same time.

Threads

Sam Collins was in the Beta Club. It didn't take a genius to figure out why Macy wouldn't want to have to be somewhere else instead.

"I'm not really sure I knew what atheism was before," Macy admitted. "Maybe I'm an agnostic. You know, someone who isn't sure there is a God but who doesn't rule it out. And suppose I am an agnostic," she continued, her voice speeding up. "Then I'm misleading the kids in my community!"

I couldn't think of a reply just then, but I didn't need one because Macy went on to debate the pros and cons out loud to herself. Should she come clean, come out as a not-so-certain-atheist-after-all or just complete the project as it was and just see what these kids had to say? But suppose the atheist kids somehow persuaded her—made such good arguments—that she was forced to *agree*? Oh no...

"Do you th-think... being an atheist is as bad as being a—what is it...a *satanist*?"

Threads

I reassured her that I didn't think atheism and satanism were at all the same though I didn't really know anything about either one. Macy seemed to be in almost as much inner turmoil as me. I felt sorry for the both of us too, but a little guilty in the way you feel when someone else shares your misery and you're privately glad.

"Have you joined another group yet?" I asked.

"Well, I like this one for people of color who live in mostly white communities," she said. And, while I'd never thought this might bother Macy, I'm now thinking perhaps it does.

"That sounds really good, Macy," I said. "I've not ever thought about you being in that situation before."

"Well, I don't really think about it... much," she said. "What are you doing?"

"Quilting with Sarah. Her mom's going to help us with the sewing." And when I said it, it sounded like such a combination of run-of-the-mill and run-for-your-life that we both cracked up.

Threads

"I think I'll stay in the belief-challenged minority," she said, letting out a good Macy guffaw.

By now, I was struggling to keep my eyes open and my limbs were nearly numb. My mind was still racing in circles.

I rolled out my yoga mat, lit my vanilla lavender soy candle and lay down in savasana pose. For the record, it's also called corpse, though it kind of gives me the creeps. I closed my eyes.

When I opened them, the candle was a puddle and morning sun beamed harsh and high through my windows.

You know when you wake up after a hard sleep and have a vague feeling like something bad happened, but you can't remember what it was? You think for a moment that maybe nothing is wrong because you're still fuzzy, then you suddenly remember and the problem seems to crash down on your shoulders all over again?

Threads

This was that kind of moment. The fight on my community... BostonBaked...

The clock. Eight o'clock already. I was running so late, I'd be lucky to get to first period on time. Tardy number three. So much for spending lunch web-surfing in the library.

Saturday was my car day, so I got to drive over to Sarah's at my own leisure. Everybody was gone. When I peeked into the garage, I saw Dad's golf clubs were gone, as were Nick's amp and stuff. Maybe Dad had dropped him off at the Scheins' or maybe a Schein had come by and picked him up. Jon would be at work.

It was nice to have the house to myself on a Saturday. My brain had rearranged the past few days' events so that Bright was resting pleasantly on the top.

We'd talked about six or seven times since BostonBaked had appeared. It was so nice not to be in the shade of a gloomy subject like Motherless Children all the time. Aside from worrying about his home situation, Bright seemed normal and he was beyond attractive too of course. His Ultimate Frisbee season began soon. "It gets me out of the house and into the fresh air. Man, I hate winter. Everything is worse when I'm all cooped up."

Sadly, I had to delete all the IM's, and the snapchats automatically evaporated into the ether or wherever self-destructing texts go. I couldn't even go over our past conversations because we had to be so careful. But I found I preferred to talk live to Bright anyway and not have to try to express everything in writing. When I'm trying to get to know someone, I would rather talk straight to them.

Plus, it seemed more like real dating.

I was also aware that I was not permitting myself to question an involvement with someone who might be going into hiding at a moment's notice. I just liked him. He was one hundred percent more interesting than other boys I knew. He was totally cute and he couldn't help his home life.

And I knew he could understand mine, even as he was careful not to ask too many questions (like I asked him).

And that was that.

When I got to Sarah's, I parked on the side street as usual. Driveways are scarce in this part of Charleston, which is near the Battery and proper garages all but unheard of. Their tiny lawns creep perilously close to the street. I could hear Mr. Goddard, Sarah's dad, the moment I cut the Volvo's motor.

"I still don't see why I shouldn't be able to install insulated glass into my own windows," Mr. Goddard was saying to a man who was wearing a gray tweed sport coat, a candy-cane striped tie and wrinkled khakis.

Mr. Goddard was wearing a Ragg wool slouchy beanie his wife or Sarah probably made, which in turn made him look ridiculously young. Mrs. Goddard has always had what Aunt Margot calls a "matronly look," with a tight perm no one else has anymore. She wore it that way before the chemo, I mean. But her husband is a total babyface. Or maybe each of them exaggerates the other.

Regardless, adults with that youthful look shouldn't wear slouchy beanies. Fashion truth.

"Brandon, it's the way the light reflects off the glass into the neighboring windows," the other man was saying. He would be with city codes or maybe with the BOAR, which stands for the Board of Architectural Review. The BOAR can literally stop you from painting your own house mid-brush stroke or adding trim work or even a row of shrubbery without their consent. They closely examine every single feature of the house to make sure it remains one hundred percent historically accurate.

To say they're like the house police is describing it pretty well.

"Do you actually think anyone notices reflections in windows?" Mr. Goddard challenged.

Threads

"Well, yes, they do. Plus, it's a codes problem Brandon. There's not one thing I can do about that, okay?"

"Even if it adds value to our home, making it more energy efficient and better for the environment?"

"Brandon, nothing adds value to an historic home like yours except what you do to preserve it exactly the way it looked when it was built. You know this. We went through this last time with the front door issue."

Mr. Goddard gestured to the road. "Oh yeah, I can't modernize my windows but the street in front of the house can be asphalt instead of dirt or cobblestone."

"That's because yours is a private residence. Personally, I wish they'd go back to crushed oyster shell roads. I mean, the raw materials are there after every oyster roast. But that's ancient history and it's up to the city…"

"So the city can't fix their potholes, but I have to maintain their damned historic landmark for them." Mr.

Threads

Goddard ripped off the slouchy beanie and threw it on the grass. He looked just like a six-foot-tall two-year-old throwing a tantrum. I half expected him to start stomping on the hat. "God, I'm sick of this town," he said instead, as the codes guy backed away to his own car.

I waved. "Oh, hello, Emily Amber," Mr. Goddard said as soon as he saw me, his face reddening. "Sorry you had to, er, witness that. Those people really drive me nuts sometimes. I mean, there's not an iota of common sense involved. It's all just rote, whatever's written on an old piece of paper."

I like Mr. Goddard. I like people who try to improve old things and are clever about it. "We call the BOAR the Hysterical Society at home," I offered while skipping up the front steps to the porch which was freshly painted a bright shiny gray. On the far end, two sawhorses stood side by side, bearing what must be the double-paned windows in question.

Threads

Sarah swung open the door before I could knock. "Hurry in! It's freezing out there and it's worse because all the front windows are popped out."

She led me into the breakfast nook where a white deluxe-looking sewing machine waited on a black trestle table. Next to it stood an impressive pile of baby clothes. I heard doors rhythmically opening and closing directly over our heads.

"Mother's scouring the house for all my baby things," Sarah explained. "Emily Amber, did you read up on the quilt group project yet?" When I looked clueless, she said, "We're making quilts using recycled clothes. Actually, I could probably make a series of quilts with all this stuff."

Out of nowhere, I hugged her. I'm not sure why. I've always said I'm not a hugger, especially not a spontaneous one. I was just happy today—happy to be out and about with the car and happy to be spending time with my oldest friend on a clear, cold day. I was happy to learn how to make something and happy Mrs. Goddard was upstairs instead of hovering over us.

Mostly, I was just happy to belong to a group other than the Motherless Child Project today.

Since I was obviously nowhere in gathering my materials, we decided I would help Sarah get started with her project that day. That way, I'd know what to do later. I turned down her offer to use some of her clothes for my project. "I'll just go to Thrift-Eze to fill in any blanks if need be," I said.

We each took a handful of clothing to start with. As we got started cutting, it soon came out in our conversation that Sarah too had an ethical problem on her hands.

"My community members are in a big argument," she said sadly. Snip, snip.

Mrs. Goddard had finally caved to the project, as long as she could join and Sarah kept all her posts public with no private messaging. "God only knows who those people really are," she'd said.

"What are they arguing about?" I asked, secretly glad I wasn't the only one hosting a community grown hostile.

"Somebody started a thread saying knitting isn't vegan," Sarah said with a big sigh, smoothing a square on her knee.

"Knitting needles aren't animal products, are they?"

"Well, no, not unless they're whale bone or something," Sarah answered. She paused.

"But...?" I prompted.

Sarah explained that some vegans don't approve of shearing wool from sheep because the wool is spun into thread to make yarn.

"Doesn't it make the sheep more comfortable when it's hot, though?" I asked.

"It's like eating honey or eggs. Some people think it's exploiting the bees and the chickens."

Threads

"Even if the bees and the chickens are going to make honey and lay eggs anyway?" Veganism seemed a tricky business.

"We can't keep the creatures from exploiting themselves, but we can avoid taking advantage," Sarah said soberly.

I didn't have the mental space to try to process that. A truth was lurking in the back of my mind as I carefully cut blocks out of the wispy-thin baby dresses—soft white, pale yellow, pink, and light blue, with tiny tucks and pleats and smocking like doll clothes.

10

Baby Things

Here's that truth: I'd never seen any of my own baby clothes. I mean, not one shred. Not one square. Not even a bib or a burp cloth. Obviously, I was a baby once. But although there were pictures of Nick and Jon and me from about toddler age, you'd never know there'd ever been a baby girl in my household.

I'll bet by now you're wondering if I'm crazy, and that I'm going to reveal my mother was an alien, and I was a foundling or a human plant she dumped with this unsuspecting human family before zipping off into space again.

Baby Things

While it's true I do feel like an alien sometimes, I'm not crazy. I'm certified sane by the Hall Institute of South Carolina, for now anyway. The real answer is a lot more complicated than that scenario. Although, it would make a cool story, and even be somewhat preferable to the truth.

This is what my history teacher Mrs. Black would call "a watershed moment," which means a critical turning point. It's what I've come to call "dry drowning." This is where it struck me full-force in the gut that not only was there no evidence of a mother, there was no evidence of her infant daughter either. It was the first time, with many to follow, I felt like I was suffocating on dry land, with plenty of air to go around.

I was glad Sarah was too swept up in her own worries and crafting to notice me having a hard time catching my breath. I tried to deep breathe in the drafty room, the blistering cool searing my lungs. The little space heater buzzing at our feet was of little help. I made myself focus on how economically and perfectly Sarah snipped out each square of carefully preserved babyhood, adding to her growing pastel stack, like fairy patches.

For lunch, Sarah made minestrone soup dotted with homemade croutons. Since it was just cold inside as out, we took our lunch out on the front porch and sat in the wicker rocking chairs. They were painted Charleston green, which is like near-black, matching the shutters. I wondered if the BOAR had jurisdiction over chairs on the porch too.

We watched Mr. Goddard measure and remeasure the new windows, even carefully take one off a sawhorse and ease it into the huge hole where the old window had been. He shook his head and murmured something to himself, oblivious to us. I could tell he was trying to weigh reason against reality. That feeling was becoming all too familiar to me.

I'd just started telling Sarah about Bright and how crazy my community was becoming when the front door

Baby Things

swung open. Sarah narrowly missed her mouth with her soup spoon.

Mrs. Goddard held a sweetgrass basket bearing yet more baby things. Her hair had already grown back a couple of inches since her cancer went into remission. It was now a grayish-brown, matchstick-straight, but it looked better than her former fried-and-dyed look.

"Emily Amber, it's been ages," she said, her voice completely devoid of inflection. Most anyone in Charleston can at least fake excitement at seeing someone. Mrs. Goddard doesn't have the gift though. I could tell she could have easily gone several more ages before seeing me again.

"I thought you might use these burp cloths as backing, Sarah," she said to her daughter. "It keeps to the theme. Emily Amber, you're so resourceful yourself, I'll bet you can make something from your Thrift-Eze finds."

See? She just *assumed* I didn't have any baby clothes.

But that's how I always react to Mrs. Goddard. Her very presence automatically puts me on the defensive. "Thanks, I've got something cool in mind," I lied. I slurped the last spoonful of soup and wished she'd go away.

Instead, Mrs. Goddard said, "You tell your handsome daddy hello. And we'll see him at the Mandatory Shared Parenting meeting next weekend."

I had no idea what Mandatory Shared Parenting was, but I knew "we" meant Mrs. Goddard by herself. She, not her husband, was deeply involved in all the parenting groups along with my dad. I sometimes wondered if my dad was the main draw for her. I didn't think Mrs. Goddard would present a temptation on his part although he seemed to really like her.

"Sarah's having a challenging time with her group," Mrs. Goddard went on. "I just don't think it's healthy to invite… strangers… into your life, especially regarding something you're passionate about. What did you decide for your personal project, dear?" She might as well have said "bitch."

"I, uh, am still working on it," I said. As if I would ever utter a word about anything—much less my community—to Mrs. Goddard. I might as well just sit down and tell my dad about it myself.

That was never gonna happen.

I got home around four, numb in my fingers from crafting and stiff from being cold most of the day, but feeling deeply satisfied from being creative. A hot bath lit with aromatherapy candles would make life divine. Both Sarah and Macy had dates tonight, but I didn't mind not having one myself. Although I remained elusive to my friends about my current love interest—something unusual, because we'd always tried to beat one other to crush confessions—I had Bright now.

Dad was in the livingroom having a drink with Mr. Rutledge, who he golfs with when Mr. Rutledge invites him to the Country Club of Charleston. That's the club for townies. Dad was raised Upstate. He came to Charleston by way of Atlanta. So he's not a true Charlestonian. Not by Charleston standards. Heck, this is the only place I remember living, and I'm not really a Charlestonian. Not in spirit, anyway.

Mr. Rutledge also goes to our church. Of all the prissy people in Charleston—and believe me, there are a lot—Mr. Rutledge is near the top of the list. He looks like he lives in the pages of *Garden & Gun*. He wears custom-made clothing from Berlin's, has this nasally-thin voice, and a mega-preppy wife named Bip (for real) whom he seems to try to avoid. I never see the two of them together, not even at church. I'm not even sure Bip is an Episcopalian.

At church, Mr. Rutledge even sits with his parents in their family pew like an overgrown kid. Though Mr. Rutledge is about Dad's age, his children are younger than us, in Lower or Intermediate School at Ashley Hall.

Baby Things

Word has it Mr. Rutledge's kids, Spencer and Margaret Anne, are "last-chance" kids for Bip, who Mr. Rutledge married when they were in their late 30's. Lots of people say Mr. Rutledge is gay. Maybe Bip too. And you know, that's cool and all. But get this—Mr. Rutledge's name, or names, I mean? *John Gay*. Seriously. Around here, if your name is John, people think you need a second name to go with it, like John David or John Mitchell. Just John isn't enough, unless you spell it Jon, like my dad and my brother. So everyone has always called Mr. Rutledge John Gay. His mother refers to him as "Our John Gay."

O.M.G.

I personally don't care who's gay or not. I know gay kids at school, like Phillip Reynolds, and the only response to his coming out last year was disappointment on the part of the girls, particularly his longtime girlfriend. No one, certainly not me, cares who anyone wants to date, marry, or have children with. But while I

Baby Things

know Gay is obviously a family name, actively using it for a man like Mr. Rutledge just seems wrong.

If Dad hung around with him more often, I'd kind of worry, but Dad has had his share of girlfriends over the years. From my point of view, Mr. Rutledge is strictly being used for his elite country club membership. I don't know what Mr. Rutledge is using Dad for. Maybe he just thinks Dad is good looking and funny in his sarcastic way. Lots of people do.

"Hello, Miss Em'ly Ambuh," Mr. Rutledge drawled. His words dripped like movie-theater butter. "You're lookin' cute as a button, and big as a minute."

Ick. "Uh. Thanks, Mr. Rutledge." I looked around for the best escape route.

"What've you got there?" Dad asked me, just making conversation, gesturing toward the blue canvas Kicks 96.2 shopping bag I'd won at a radio event at Citadel Mall one year. I use it for my Thrift-Eze and other shopping trips.

Baby Things

I'd brought home a few quilting squares from Sarah's as patterns for whatever I was going to manage to find for mine. I pulled out a handful to show Dad.

And I don't know what prompted me to say it, or if I just felt bold with Mr. Rutledge sitting there, but I just blurted out the burning question.

"Hey Dad, do I have any baby clothes?"

Dad almost choked on his drink. "Baby clothes?" he sputtered as if I'd said, "Hooker clothes?"

"I just need some for this quilting project we're doing," I explained, knowing full well I'd totally baited my dad. But I couldn't help it. I wanted to know. "I never saw any. I just wondered." I shrugged, trying to act casual.

"My mama would have a coronary if it were proposed that we cut up any of the infant clothes," Mr. Rutledge broke in. "A coronary. Some of them have been in my fam'ly for genuhrations."

Baby Things

Finally, Dad's mind must have latched onto something because he stood up quickly. "Wait here, Emily Amber. I think I know of…something."

I waited with my bag of baby scraps, avoiding nosy questions from Mr. Rutledge by asking him about how his daughters were liking Ashley Hall and if he and Bip were going to keep them there or send them to public high school like us.

A good ten minutes later, Dad reappeared with an odd look on his face, ashamed almost. He held a small stained blue and white striped Mickey Mouse baseball shirt with big white snaps on the front. It was obviously not a baby shirt—maybe a toddler size. I know my sizing from sifting through thrift stores all the time.

"Jonathan, now what would a baby girl do wearin' that?" Mr. Rutledge asked. Dad's mouth tightened. I knew he wanted to tell Mr. Rutledge to shut up. Or worse.

"You know how it goes," Dad said instead, an edge in his voice. "Baby things get ruined. Emily Amber, you were the messiest, most active child on this earth. Wore out everything you didn't ruin. That's why you mainly wore your brothers' hand-me-downs."

I knew this couldn't possibly be true. Everything? Sarah's mom might be at the extreme clothes-saving end of the spectrum, but most people had *something*. A blanket, a baby shoe, a bib. Some unused shower or christening gift. Apparently, Dad had kept Jon's or Nick's crusty toddler baseball jersey, even though the item was sad in itself.

"Did I maybe have a blanket or something I liked?" I pressed, egged on by Mr. Rutledge's close attention to the conversation.

"Uh… hey, wait. There might be something along those lines in the linen closet. I was thinking of clothing. Let me go check." Even if I was going to catch hell later for making Dad look bad, it was nice to feel in charge for a little bit. Since I'd started my project, something inside me had shifted or emerged, or something. I'd realized I was not only Jonathan Ross's daughter. I was someone else's daughter. Maybe I'd never know whose, but I knew I was tired of not knowing who I was in my own house.

For some reason, the realization that I wasn't one hundred percent Jonathan Ross's daughter made me realize that there was more to me.

Dad disappeared again, this time returning with a grubby little pillow. I recognized it from the back of the linen closet, where it had been wedged as long as I could remember, usually obscured by a stack of towels and washcloths our weekly cleaning lady Dorothea put away. It was one of those things you just ignored, assuming it was someone else's or there for some purpose. Too ratty to actually use, but not ragged enough to throw out.

Dad looked a little embarrassed as he handed it to me. Mr. Rutledge jiggled his drink glass, seemingly unimpressed.

I took the little pillow and peered at its filthy casing. "I'm going to go wash this," I said. "Thanks, Dad."

"Sacrificin' the family history over a school project," Mr. Rutledge mumbled. He drew a long sip of scotch or bourbon or whatever he was drinking. "That's why I'm keepin' my daughters in a proper private school."

11

Hidden Words

I ran a warm, shallow bath in my bathroom sink and added a capful of Ivory Snow, which I use to wash my vintage and handmade stuff. I carefully tugged the crusty-edged case off the pillow, pressed it gently into the suds. The case appeared to be very fine linen, threadbare in places, but sewn well and otherwise intact. Maybe if it cleaned up okay, I could base a quilt around it. Or a fresher pillow. Or something.

Since seeing Sarah's pile of baby memories, I longed to have at least one of my own. I needed to see evidence that I was a baby once, even if it was just a filthy scrap.

The pillow stuffing that had been inside was mashed nearly flat with a sharp brown corner poking out of a corner seam. I left it on the counter for now.

While I let the pillow case soak, I decided to check my community and see if I'd heard from Bright.

BostonBaked was back. Mr. Neil had told me I would be able to block him, but not yet, because the national technical committee for the project was tracking BostonBaked's IP address. He never had registered to the community, so there wasn't any other information about him.

Mr. Neil told me I was free to say anything or nothing, but to be careful not to fall into the trap of arguing with BostonBaked, because that was clearly what he wanted.

Hidden Words

BOSTONBAKED: I wasn't going to spend any more time worrying about why you kids are pie-in-the-sky pining for mothers who have been proven—PROVEN—to be unfit. But as a caring parent and Father myself, I thought maybe I'd try and help you by sharing some information that can get you on the right track. Check out this website written by Yours Truly—and see if it can't do more for you than this little school project. Ember, I know you've tried to do a good job gathering these kids together. But it really is a formula for disaster in the hands of someone who is obviously in deep water and in way over her own head. You need some guidance, not just a bunch of clueless kids complaining to one another that their mothers aren't "allowed" in their lives. All the misinformation you're trading back and forth is downright dangerous.

And by the way, my condolences to those who've lost their mothers to illness or something other than our Family Court System.

But I urge all of you to check out www.father-ledfamilies.us. There are many articles about how Fathers have been cheated of the opportunity to raise their own children and there's also an historical look at the importance of Fathers as Heads of Household. Except for a time in the mid-1900s, Fathers had the final say-so on where and how their children lived. For a time, there was a trend of mothers receiving custody, but it was because Fathers had more opportunities to earn a better living, so many of them allowed the mother to retain custody. Then the courts continued this trend until we decided the time was right to reclaim our rights to parent our own children our way and without interference from the mother or the government.

Somehow over time, it became a sentiment that children need their biological mothers throughout their entire lives. All that "baseball, mom and apple pie" stuff is just greeting card sentimentality. The mothers you might see on sitcoms and in movies aren't anything like real mothers. (Just read any magazine to see what those actresses are really like! Entitled attention-hogs all of them, especially those who strut around to show off their children or involve them in nasty custody wars.)

Hidden Words

The image of the caring, concerned mother is a myth. Fathers know best, and they can be an as good or better nurturing presence in a child's life as any mother. That's the cold, hard truth. I know Fathers who attend to their children's needs in the most tender and loving ways. Believe me, it's a beautiful thing to see.

I take it all of you on here don't have a mother in your lives for one reason or another, so there's no way you can know this. I just want to offer you a little food for thought: Don't you think it's possible you have it better as a child in a Father-only household than those who don't?

MOL38: Mr. Baked, my dad raised me to be kind to others so I won't say what I want to. Plus, I don't want to get a bad grade. But my mother died. I don't like you saying she wasn't important. She was, and my dad thought so too! She was our whole world. We miss her every day. She did so much for our family. We would give anything to have her back.

BOSTONBAKED: Mol, I certainly didn't intend my remarks toward intact families, with a Father and a mother. Indeed, that is the perfect household. I'm directing my posts to the misguided who think that the court system somehow awards custody to the wrong person. My condolences. Perhaps you'd like to share my website with your Father.

…

MOL38: I don't think I want to show him. He isn't like you. He misses my mother. She was a lot more than what you say a mother is. After she died, he didn't know what to do. He had to learn all kinds of things. It was very hard on him and all of us.

BOSTONBAKED: Bless him, it sounds like your Father is doing an excellent job and I'm sorry for your loss. Sometimes the best thing a single Father can do on his own is hire some help. Do you help around the house too? Do you have chores?

Though Mr. Neil had said I didn't need to mediate and warned me about arguing, I just couldn't let this go on. It was my community.

ME: BostonBaked, I'm the moderator of this forum and I don't like how you're making my members feel. This community isn't for you. It's for the kids. Why do you think mothers aren't necessary? Do you have a mother?

Hidden Words

BOSTONBAKED: *Sometimes the truth hurts. I'm just merely trying to point you in the right direction. Everything we do is #FortheKids, to #PreservetheFamily, for the #NeedsofKids. I'm trying to help you not look ridiculous, but I can't save you from your own ignorance. Incidentally, does your own Father know about your project? I don't know what your story is. I just jumped in where I saw an opportunity to educate, but I'd be curious to know.*

And yes, to answer your question. I hope you don't mind that I had a chuckle over it. I have a mother, who even as a co-breadwinner manages to perfectly attend to the needs of my Father and our family. She remains very supportive of all I do to promote the preservation of Fatherhood.

…..

…..

Ping. IM.

BRIGHT: *Hey Ember. You've got to get rid of this guy BostonBaked.*

ME: *I know. I don't understand what he's trying to do. I told my teacher though. They're tracking him first.*

Hidden Words

BRIGHT: *Oh, I do. Know what he's doing I mean. These websites he talks about? Totally Fathers' Rights. They have nothing to do with what's good for the kids. My dad is into FR bigtime.*

ME: *What is Fathers' Rights really? I don't get it.*

BRIGHT: *It's a hate group that pretends not to be and fools a lot of people. It's not guys who want to be good dads. That's their front. Their real goal is to take kids from their mothers so they won't have to pay child support and can continue to torture the moms and control kids' lives after the divorce. It's bad news. Trust me. That's why I'm here.*

ME: *My dad is in lots of parenting groups, but I don't think it's like that one. I mean, he's a single parent and he wants to do a good job. My friend's mom is in some of the same groups. One is about joint parenting or something like that. A sharing thing. I was thinking maybe that single parents get together and help each other. I don't know why my dad would be involved in divorced parent stuff, unless he's helping people.*

....

ME: *I mean, if the parents share, that's good, right?*

BRIGHT: Uh no. It just sounds good. If it's Shared Parenting or Mandatory Shared Parenting, that is a product of the same Fathers' Rights people. A movement. They want people, mainly the moms, to go for it by pretending it's fair. It's a bait and switch. They get the mothers to agree and to think it's their only option, and then in time they use it against them and often gain full custody. Slippery slope.

ME: That's the word. My friend's mom said a Mandatory Shared Parenting meeting. I don't think my dad is one of those bad ones though. Like the Fathers' Rights or whatever. I mean, he's not a bad dad.

BRIGHT: I don't know anything except what you tell me. If you say he's a good dad, then he is. I'm just glad to know you. I don't want anything bad to ever happen to you.

I loved talking to Bright. I could tell him everything—maybe because he was in on my big secret I was keeping from my dad about my community. We talked about normal stuff too. After we had switched to cell phones that day so we could talk more easily, I told him about the quilting project and Sarah's clothes and about how my dad came up with crap when I asked him for mine. It was really starting to bother me.

"What do you think about that?" I asked Bright. "That I have no baby records or anything? There's not a book or a rattle or anything that I've ever seen."

I'd asked Dad about a baby book years ago when everyone was going through theirs and looking for early family pics for a family history project. There were no books—just an old Christmas card photo of Dad and us three kids and various pics from Upstate with my cousins. I made copies of them and made a collage. Dad filled out the form that went with the project.

"That's hard to say, babe," Bright said.

Wait a minute. Babe?

Even though he couldn't see me, I mechanically raked my fingers through my hair, suddenly self-conscious, but thrilled.

"Uh well, I'd better go get that pitiful pillowcase out of the rinse. I think it could tear into pieces if you look at it wrong."

"Hey, let me know how that goes and show it to me later, okay?" Bright asked. Pause. "Listen, I wish we could maybe get together like normal," he said. "I really do."

"Me too," I said and shivered.

I went back to check on the pillow case in the sink. The water around it was filthy, the detergent bubbles clinging frothy gray to the edges. I drained the dirty water and ran a little warm water over the material to get the rest out. I carefully picked up the case with my thumbs and forefingers.

I could now see a trace of a pattern on the case, little light blue X's: like one of those stamped-pattern cross stitch kits you see in Jo-Ann Fabrics or Michaels.

About half the threads were gone and the ones left were faded pastels—blue, golden tan and pink. The X's were all neatly worked. There was a picture: Winnie the Pooh and Piglet holding hands. Each clutched a yellow flower in the free hand.

Hidden Words

Below it were carefully embroidered words in dark brown. They were neat but not quite uniform, as if added to the design as an afterthought: *If there ever comes a day when we can't be together, keep me in your heart. I'll stay there forever... Winnie the Pooh*

Tears puddled in my eyes, blurring the image and the words. A sting of recognition. Had I seen this before? I had, I knew I had. If my mind didn't recognize it, something deep inside me did.

Wiping the tears away with my Oxford shirt sleeve, I rolled up the pillowcase carefully in a clean towel to absorb what was left of the moisture. I pressed on it gently and rolled it out again. The piece was nearly dry since the material was so thin.

I laid it out on the counter to let it dry thoroughly before I tried to figure out what I might do with it. I picked up the flat, battered cushion that had been inside the case.

There was really nothing to it since the fill was coming out, so I tugged on it a little more until the seam split wide open. I drew out the grimy square and peeled back a couple of layers to see what it was made of. There was no saving this.

Still, I peeled one more layer, which revealed a square piece of cloth that was preserved, sandwiched in the foam. It was not a linen, but a light cotton, still white. There were words on it, written by hand in midnight blue ink. The neat print slanted slightly left.

I sank to the floor, pressing my back against the counter, to read:

My Precious Emily Amber,

As I write this, you have just turned three. I wonder how old you will be when you find my message. You love your Winnie the Pooh pillow so much. I mean you did... I mean I don't know if you still do or not because I don't know how old you are now. This is so hard... Anyway, that's why I decided to hide my letter to you in your baby pillow. I have no idea how many years will have passed by the time you find

this, or if you ever will. But if you're reading right now, please know that I did not abandon you or your brothers. I did not give my babies away. I would never ever do that. I love you all more than life. I pray God will keep you safe. If you know Lilah Schein, please ask her about me. She will have the answers you need to understand why we were separated.

With All My Love,

Mom

P.S. This is my favorite quote, which I will remember you by always, and I hope you'll like it too: "In one of the stars I shall be living. In one of them I shall be laughing. And so it will be as if all the stars were laughing, when you look at the sky at night… You — only you — will have stars that can laugh!"
— Antoine de Saint-Exupéry, The Little Prince

12

Patterns

I stared at the letter for so long that it seemed to become part of the pattern of black and white tiles on the wall. I was sitting full on the floor now, legs splayed out in front of me, limp as a doll— like that time weeks ago in Thrift-Eze.

Except this had to be a dream. I was not awake. I couldn't be. Right?

At Thrift-Eze, I'd been upset, frustrated and sad because I suddenly missed a mother I didn't have. I wanted her to save me.

Now I was holding a letter from her.

But, who was she?

Patterns

I read the fabric letter again and again, waiting for the letters and words to rearrange into something that made sense. What I'd read before had to be a trick of the mind or of the light.

But the words didn't change no matter how long I stared at them.

Please know that I did not abandon you or your brothers. I did not give my babies away... If you know Lilah Schein, please ask her about me.

Suddenly, Taylor Swift's high-pitched voice broke the silence in my bathroom. Her voice seemed to ping off the tiles. Startled, I listened to the full range of lyrics of Haunted, which was my current favorite song. The song stopped. Then it began again. I have no idea how many times the phone rang before I picked up.

It was Nick. "Hello? You there?"

I'm not sure if I'd even said "hello." I just couldn't speak. I felt like a ghost in one of those stories—where it wants to warn somebody of something but no words come out because it has no voice.

Patterns

I'm kind of fascinated by ghosts. Not only do I live in a town that actually brags about its haunted places and gives tours of them, but I love the idea of different planes of existence where people who pass on might not really go away at all.

"Em? You okay?"

I didn't intend to be rude, but because I couldn't summon any words, I thought it more polite to just hang up.

The phone rang again.

"Hey Ember, I don't know what's going on, but I need the car tonight for a gig. I'm filling in for the house bass player at Shucker's."

"Em? You there?"

Finally, some words found their way into the receiver.

"I found… something."

Silence. Then Nick asked, "You found something? What?"

"A note. A pillow. A… from Mom."

Patterns

Silence.

"I d-don't… know.. what this… is."

"Em, I'm not sure what you're talking about, but you don't sound like yourself."

That's because I may not be myself.

"I'm on my way home in about twenty minutes," he continued. "We've got to run through a couple more songs. Then I'll get Scotty to drop me off, okay? And if you have to go somewhere, I can take you."

When Nick did get home, I was still sitting in a daze on the bathroom floor.

Without getting up, I showed him the pillowcase, the shredded insides, and the cloth letter. He stood, reading. Then he looked at me, confused. It was not a typical look for him, and I found it deeply troubling.

I also noticed that his eyes, normally a warm hazel-brown, looked almost black.

Patterns

"Are you high?" I squinted back at him, saying the first words that came to mind that had anything to do with life outside this bathroom.

"Huh? Listen, why don't we get you off this floor and into your room."

He extended his jean-jacket clad arm and helped pull me up. I immediately went to sit down again on my yoga mat.

From lotus position, I jabbed a finger at the letter Nick was still holding. "What... does it mean?"

I pulled out my aromatherapy candle and tried to light it, but my fingers were shaking. So I held the jar to my nose, breathing in vanilla lavender.

"Nick, Emily Amber," Dad called from the stairwell. I'd forgotten Dad was even here. I'd forgotten a familiar life was still here. "I'm going with John Gay to the club. Be back in a couple of hours. If you go anywhere, be back by midnight, all right? Nick, if you have a gig, it's two o'clock, tops."

Patterns

"Playing at Shucker's Dad. Filling in. No idea when I'll be done," Nick yelled back.

Dad had recently extended our curfew after we'd complained enough. As far as I knew, Jon had never been held to any curfew. Dad had instituted it for Nick when he started playing with the Wingnuts and then continued it for me. Although I'd noticed my curfew was always earlier.

My heart was pounding hearing Dad's voice. I felt like I'd been suddenly transported to some remote war zone where I couldn't see the opposing army. No wonder I couldn't manage to sit anywhere other than the floor.

"Hey, uh, Em, I need to grab something out of my room. Can I take this?" He waved the letter.

"No," I said but I didn't know why at first. Well, yes I did. The letter was mine. Because it was written to me.

To my precious Emily Amber.

Patterns

Nick handed it back to me—a little reluctantly, I thought. "I'll be back in a few."

I clutched it tightly, skimmed it I again. I realized I'd nearly memorized it.

I have no idea how many years will have passed by the time you find this. Please know that I did not abandon you or your brothers… If you know Lilah Schein, please ask her about me. She will have the answers you need to understand why we were separated.

Lilah Schein. Mrs. Schein. **If you know Lilah Schein, please ask her about me.** What would she have to do with my mother now?

But the pieces were starting to pull and snap together—like magnets or Legos long missing from their set. Mrs. Schein was the only person I knew who ever talked about me being born at all. The only person I knew who mentioned me being… a baby.

I heard a light rap on my door. "Em, if you're not doing anything, you wanta go get something to eat? I

Patterns

don't have to be at Clark's until nine thirty. I can bring you back here first, or take you wherever." Clark's is a seafood restaurant in Mt. Pleasant. Their bar stays open late on weekends. Their house band is super popular and this was a big deal to Nick, still being in high school and all.

I carefully folded my letter, meaning to put it under my mattress. But instead, I buried it deep into my jeans pocket. It had been concealed from me all those years. Now that I'd found it, I wanted to keep it close for some reason.

We went to Mellow Mushroom because it's Nick's favorite. Plus, he was buying. Usually, I avoid pizza joints and anywhere that serves mainly fattening stuff. But all I'd had to eat today was that bowl of minestrone soup at Sarah's. I could rationalize a slice of pizza and maybe even some salad. Besides, I was starving.

Nick alternated scarfing down pizza with looking about five inches to the left of my face, seemingly

Patterns

mesmerized by the psychedelic wall art. I was still wondering if he was high.

What was weirder was that he'd brought this large, bulky envelope along. It sat on the table between us like a divider. I thought maybe it contained a set list or sheet music. Whatever it was, there was a lot of it—the packet looked like it was about to split open. And, it was apparently too important to leave in the car.

I surprised myself by eating two slices of Gourmet White along with half a Greek salad. I rationalized by skipping the sweet tea and washing it all down with lemon water. I felt some energy coming back to me. Warm circulation spread through my arms and legs and tingled in my toes and fingers. They'd not completely thawed from the cold day cutting fabric at the Goddard's.

"What's in the packet?" I asked for about the fourth time. I was getting tired of looking at Nick looking at the wall.

Patterns

"Uh, nothing," Nick said. "It's… just some stuff I brought in case you might want to see it."

"Why would I want to see it?" I asked. Then, automatically I added, "I don't want to see it."

Nick took off for his gig around nine leaving me alone in the house for the second time that day. I caught myself wandering into the kitchen, tempted to grab another piece of the leftover pizza we'd brought home. *Note to self: Boredom is the gateway to diet sabotage.*

I stood in front of the closed refrigerator going through my mental "Do-I-really-need-this-food?" routine.

Before I walked away to try to occupy myself, I scanned the fridge door while reviewing my growing Pantone swatch-color chips magnet collection. I'd come up with the idea to preserve my favorite color chips on Pinterest. I'd coated the cardstock in shellac and glued magnets to the back. Right now, the magnets held up only random stuff like Jon's work and training schedules,

Patterns

the latest grocery list, instructions for Dorothea, Dad's Promise Keepers calendar and various contact numbers.

I peered at the numbers. Near the top was the Scheins', which had been jotted by Nick in his half-print, half-cursive scrawl.

If you know Lilah Schein, please ask her about me. She will have the answers you need to understand why we were separated.

Almost on auto-pilot, I picked up the kitchen phone. It's one of those way-outdated wall-mounted phones, beige spiral cord dangling from the receiver. I rarely saw anyone using that phone except for Dad, who always maintained landlines were essential in case storms or other disasters wipe out the electricity. And believe me, it happens in hurricane central.

So although he has a cell phone, he's distrustful of them and cordless ones too.

"What good does it do if you have to charge it constantly?" he'd say. "That makes it no much better than a regular phone, plus you can't find it half the time.

Patterns

Now a landline… You always know where it is. And you don't need anything to make it work."

"Unless the phone company is out too," Nick would inevitably point out.

"I think you know what I mean," Dad would retort with a scowl.

The receiver felt heavy, rubber-chunky in my hand. Looking at the contact list, I dialed the number for the Scheins'. This would be their landline as mandated by Dad. It was no good if it was for a cell phone, which could mean they were anywhere. And I knew it was only on the list to make sure Nick went where he was saying he was. I couldn't imagine Dad dialing up the Scheins directly, not even in an emergency.

I could hear my heart beating in my eardrums as I listened to the ringtone. Four, five times. "Hello, you've reached the Scheins'." It was Mrs. Schein's low, soft lilt. "We're so very sorry to have missed your call…"

I hung up.

Patterns

It was Saturday night. They could be anywhere really. I felt relieved they hadn't answered. I mean, what would I have said?

Later, I got bold and Skyped Bright. I usually waited for him to initiate a conversation but not this time. I told him about the strange note I'd found. I held it up so he could read it.

That night he seemed restless and jumpy. I mean, he was always kind of hyper but tonight he was moving around his room as we Skyped, passing in and out of the camera's eye. I couldn't tell if he was actually even listening. It was kind of annoying.

"Is something wrong?" I asked finally. "Do you want to just give me a call later? Or tomorrow… or something?"

"Oops, sorry, babe," he said. He sat down in front of the computer, looked into the camera trying to smile. His eyes looked pink-rimmed, tired. "Thanks for slowing me down. I really needed to see your pretty face."

Patterns

I rehashed about the note just in case he hadn't heard me before. Then I told him about trying to call Mrs. Schein.

"I think you're totally doing the right thing trying to find a way talk with Mrs. Schein, babe. Maybe in person. As soon as you can. Wish I could be there."

"Someone call Lilah Schein?" Dad asked me the next morning, barely looking up from the Sunday *Post and Courier*. He'd obviously been up for a while because the coffee was on, but the pot was only a quarter full. Evidently the country club evening had run late. I'd heard him come in around one a.m. when I was still talking to Bright. I'd quickly told Bright goodbye and logged off.

I decided not saying anything was riskier than answering. "Uh, why Dad?"

"She left a voicemail at two thirty a.m. and woke me from a dead sleep. That's why. She wondered who

Patterns

called her. She was worried because she saw it was our landline ringing in, but there was no message."

I shrugged. "Well, Nick must have got in fine. Volvo's in the driveway." I turned to pour myself a cup of coffee so Dad wouldn't see my reddening face.

"I told Lilah that just because her kids drink, smoke and stay out all night it doesn't mean mine do. Well, if someone did call from here, at least they were home. Must have been Nick. Oh well, not my problem."

I was planning to slip away with my coffee when Dad looked up and seemed to notice me for the first time, even though he'd been talking to me. "Hey, you're here. And, on a Sunday morning no less. How about going to church with your dear old dad for once, Emily Amber?"

I swallowed. "Um, sure. Let me go get dressed."

Church was the usual. Stand up, sit down, recite, shut up, listen, sing, sit, and stand. Don't get me wrong, the Episcopal services can be nice if a little stiff. There's

Patterns

something reassuring about knowing exactly what to expect. But, for the same reason it's boring.

Our cathedral is gorgeous with graceful arches and columns in direct contrast to the plain lines of Cross Path. As much as I love to watch the sunbeams play through the rainbow-colors in the stained glass windows, they were the same windows and the same colors every time. My church is just so *predictable*, that's all. Even the choir never changes. There's never the occasional guest soloist or musician or anything like Cross Path has.

Right now it was tempting to wish I'd gone to our church on the morning I went with Macy and heard "Sometimes I Feel Like a Motherless Child."

But I had heard it, and now I had to make good with Dad. He hadn't challenged me about the baby clothes thing. I was definitely swinging back and forth with the new and disturbing information I was finding. And, hiding my project from him was causing me major guilt mixed with terror that he'd find out.

Patterns

A secret is a burden.

And what I was learning was terrifying enough without making him into an enemy or suspicious or whatever by acting too differently. Plus, when you have only one parent, no matter what kind of parent they are, it's all you've got. You might have grandparents, aunts, uncles and cousins around as well, but it doesn't change your immediate family exactly.

I had a mother once, a mother who knew me. That was obvious now. But she was still only long-ago words on a piece of cloth.

Dad was right here. Waiting for me to get ready.

I decided to do some sucking up and a little advance damage control by going to church with Dad as much as possible. He seemed to have a solid career going with the same firm he'd always been with and he liked to go to the country club and hobnob like everyone else did.

But church? That was Dad's place to shine.

Patterns

Two Sundays later, I sat in one of the burgundy velvet-covered chairs outside the vestry office reading Episcopal Life as usual until Dad came out. He'd been made treasurer at the beginning of the year and from the amount of time he took in that office, I wondered if he had to literally count the offering himself.

"Hey Em, sorry for the wait," he said to me as he exited the room with two other sober-suited men. "Um, I thought we'd go to 64 Prince for a change."

64 Prince is one of Charleston's best restaurants. It's more of a special-occasion place than a normal Sunday brunch destination, at least for us.

I shrugged. "Okay." 64 Prince is all about Southern and seafood. After all, I had the skills to negotiate that kind of menu. It was far better than a buffet of who-knows-what, where it's difficult to ask questions about calories and fat content and such.

"I have a friend I'd like you to meet," Dad added, and I could tell by his careful effort to appear offhand that it was anything but. This would mean a new

Patterns

girlfriend gauging by the formality of our meeting place. It would be someone he'd been seeing, but hadn't introduced us to yet.

The formal setting also would be intended to foil any possibility that we wouldn't be on our best behavior. Of course with Jon working all hours or at Ashley's and Nick not having a remote interest in attending anyone's church, it was on me.

I knew the drill.

13

Snapshots

By the time we got to 64 Prince, the line wound out the door and puddled into the parking lot. I hoped Dad wouldn't insist on waiting outside since it was freezing and all I had on over my church outfit was my gray pea coat.

But it turned out his new "friend" was already waiting inside with a table claimed. She was a petite woman in a red suit with a pearl necklace gleaming pinkish against it. Her chin-length ash blond bob seemed the grownup version of the kid's standard hairdo. Green eyes peered from between navy parentheses of tattooed eyeliner.

Note to self: Never, ever tattoo anything on your face, however much you hate putting on makeup day in and day out. It will go out of style quicker than the ink dries.

Dad's choice of greeting style is the usual way we kids quickly size up the length and romantic intensity of a relationship. Instead of a kiss on the cheek or a hug, Dad merely touched this woman on the arm and gestured to me.

Oh God, this woman wasn't here for him. She was here for me.

"Emily Amber, meet Joy," Dad said, smiling. "Joy Handler."

Joy was already two-thirds of the way through a glass of white wine. Who knew how long she'd been waiting? Dad ordered a Bloody Mary. 64 Prince has a bar nearly half the size of the main dining room. I ordered a Diet Coke.

Snapshots

"Well, it's a pleasure to meet you," said Joy. "Aren't you stunning."

While we waited for our appetizers, Dad described everything about Joy except exactly why the three of us were here together. Turns out, she was a Guardian ad Litem in the Charleston County court system, which meant she was someone, in her case a lawyer, who represented children.

I remembered hearing that term, Guardian ad Litem. It was from my community—maybe from Bright. Yes, I was sure it was. His stepmother was one. He'd said she was just as bad as his dad, and maybe even worse.

"Okay," I said, trying to smile politely. I was anticipating my shrimp salad, which is on the lean menu and is awesome. I love it when a menu includes the calorie and nutritional information. It means I can actually enjoy my food without any calculating on my part.

"Joy is also leading the local effort in the Mandatory Shared Parenting movement," Dad added.

Snapshots

"Your friend Sarah's mother is on the committee with us."

"Oh," I fudged, "that's… very interesting. Shared Parenting." I leaning back a little as the waiter placed a small ivory bowl of fragrant, steaming soup in front of me. Chunks of blue crab meat peeked out of its creamy cap. Dad always orders She-Crab soup for the whole table wherever it's served, which is about half the restaurants in Charleston. It's his thing. He loves the stuff. I allow myself about five or six soup-spoonfuls. It's sinfully rich, with heavy cream and butter and sometimes even sherry and roe, which is the eggs found in the crab. It sounds gross, but it's delicious. I mean, here, we eat raw oysters. They're divine.

I tried to block out Joy's and Dad's shop talk, tuning in instead to the clatter and clang of busy brunch. Then midway through our entrees, Dad turned back to me.

"Uh, Emily Amber. Joy happens to be here specifically to meet you. She thinks you might be interested in a project that goes along with the Shared Parenting effort. Joy, want to explain?"

"Well, Shared Parenting is the wave of the future for divorcing couples," Joy said, blotting her lips with her napkin, leaving a rosy ring on the crisp white linen. I noticed burgundy tattoo lines were now showing around her mouth.

"Why?" I asked.

"Because we believe it lessens tensions and solves the problem of equal custody time for each parent."

They clearly wanted me to engage in this conversation. That's why we were here. So I said, "What about the kid? What if the kid wants to stay in one place most of the time?"

Joy shot me a practiced, patient smile. "We think the child would want to spend equal time with the parents."

"What if one parent is abusive?" I asked. Of course, I was drawing straight from the Motherless Child Project.

"In most circumstances, they're not," Joy said. "And false allegations are the biggest problem in all this."

Dad broke in, "There is a trend, especially among mothers, to make false charges against the dad to make him look bad. Shared Parenting will help improve the situation."

I thought of QueenofPink, of SoulGrrl. Of Bright. "Why do they think the charges are false?" I asked, knowing I was dancing on the line. "I mean, how do they know?" I reasoned that Joy was on my nerves and they had no business ambushing me over lunch anyway.

"Because the mothers want control," Joy said. "Even if the father has maybe been a less than a proper husband, it shouldn't mean he should suffer isolation from his children."

"But, if he's mean to the mom, he might be mean to his kids," I said.

I could tell I was getting to Joy. She was looking around for the waiter again. "If he is, it's probably because his marriage is bad," she said, her ink-laced lips tightening. "It takes two to make a marriage. And there are many federally funded programs to help the fathers learn to be… better fathers."

"Who helps the mothers?"

I couldn't believe I was doing this. It was like someone had taken charge of my mouth and was operating it for me. But, there was no turning back. I put my fork down and reached into my pocket just to touch the fabric letter. I carried it with me all the time now. Not only did I not want to let anyone else get ahold of it, it felt like a talisman—a note from the past to my present. I still hadn't gotten around to trying to talk to Mrs. Schein. I just wasn't sure how I was going to do that yet, but I'd certainly not forgotten about my mother's message.

"Emily Amber, the last thing those mothers need is help with their… shenanigans." Joy's voice was sharp by now. She drained the rest of her wine and glanced around again.

Snapshots

"What if the kid wants to be with her—I mean his or her mother?"

"A child is not qualified to make that decision," Joy said haughtily. "And, Emily Ann…"

"Amber," Dad and I corrected her at once.

"Emily Amber, this Shared Parenting plan is what is best and fairest for all parties. It ensures the fathers—I mean, both parents—have equal access to the child. It keeps the fathers from having to pay inordinate amounts of money or any money at all to the mother simply because she's female. It neutralizes allegations of abuse."

"What if the mother doesn't have any money? Like, if she was a stay-home mom?" Lots of my friends' parents had this arrangement, including the Goddards.

"Emily Amber, if she's any kind of self-respecting human being," Joy said, and I could tell she was really rattled now because she'd chewed off the rest of her lipstick, "she will."

And then it struck me who she sounded like—who they both sounded like.

They sounded like BostonBaked.

A coil of anger formed in my stomach.

I had a sudden idea—an inspiration—the kind that if you thought about it for two seconds, you'd choose not to say it. I said it.

"Splitting the... baby... This all sounds kind of like that King Solomon Bible story."

Joy smiled suddenly. "Exactly!" Dad looked relieved.

"Except one of those two women fighting over the baby wanted to cut the baby in half. King Solomon realized she couldn't be the real mother to want to harm the baby like that, so he knew who the real mother was."

Thank you, Vacation Bible School.

"This isn't about mothers," Dad interrupted, setting his napkin in front of his plate signaling brunch was over. "This is about *fathers*."

Snapshots

"If it's 'shared parenting,' why is it just about the fathers?"

"Well, Emily Amber, it's been a pleasure meeting you," Joy said hurriedly. "You are as… inquisitive and… sharp… as your daddy described. And, I hope you don't mind that your father has placed me on retainer in case you need any of my services." She set her cloth napkin on the table in front of her—red lipstick was smeared all over it. If I didn't know better I'd have thought it was a crime scene.

"I don't even have a mother," I said in my innocent voice, which I usually accompany with a little shrug. "I mean, who'd be fighting over me?"

Joy and Dad exchanged puzzled glances.

"No one, dear," Joy said tersely. "Jon, thank you so much, but I really have to go. I need to prep for our meeting this afternoon. See you there?"

"Absolutely," Dad said and in a last-ditch effort to save the conversation added, "Uh, Joy… before you go, did you want to ask Emily Amber about the side project?

Interviewing children to talk about the importance of a father's role in the life of a child?"

"I'd have to think on it some more. I'm not certain it's the best… fit… after all." She stood, gathered her coat and purse and walked out of the restaurant, swaying the slightest bit. Her heels clicked on the polished floor as she blended into the knot of people at the entrance.

I noticed she'd left Dad with the tab. I guessed that was part of their retainer deal.

After we got home, I immediately ran up to my room and got in a hot shower to hide from Dad, who was plenty perturbed at me. A few times in the car riding home, he'd opened his mouth as if to say something, then closed it again as if unable to form the words he wanted to say.

I washed my hair twice and tried out my new Aveda deep-treatment conditioner to stall for more time. When I absolutely had to get out because the hot water was gone, I wrapped myself in one of my grosgrain-edged towels—another DIY project—swept my wet hair into a turban with another and sat on the side of the tub to think.

Everything seemed to be congealing into a big mess. There was my site, which was still in limbo until we could get rid of BostonBaked. I knew I needed help. I was almost afraid to check on my community at this point. Certainly I'd done more work on it already than most other kids were doing. I just hadn't realized what a rabbit hole my topic would be. Piecing together my own life was becoming difficult enough.

Then, I was seriously crushing on a boy I'd never seen in person, who had more problems than anyone I'd ever met. He was someone I sensed was dangerous, not because of who he was but because of the people around him.

Most strangely, I'd received a highly troubling message from a woman, someone who made even Nick nervous. Dad was sufficiently suspicious from my baby clothes inquiries that he hired an attorney to do what exactly? Save me from myself?

And then there was that mini-argument I'd instigated in the restaurant. I'd been raised to not ask questions, to not argue with adults and authority figures. It didn't quite stop me from doing it at times, but this was two back-to-back occurrences of being out of line with Dad. There was the time with Mr. Rutledge a couple of weeks ago while putting Dad on the spot about the baby things and then with this Joy person. Which was laying it on really thick.

My eyes came to rest on the little pillowcase, which now lay dry and limp beside the sink. I picked it up and moved my fingers lightly over the careful pastel stitches.

If there ever comes a day when we can't be together, keep me in your heart. I'll stay there forever… Winnie the Pooh

Snapshots

I got dressed and waited to make sure Dad had left for that Shared Parenting meeting. Seconds after he backed out in the Beamer, I was beating on Nick's door.

He answered, looking half asleep and exhausted. "What is it, Ember?"

"That envelope," I said. "That one you brought to Mellow Mushroom that night. I want to see it."

"The one you repeatedly said you didn't want to see?" But Nick groggily padded over to the pair of jeans he'd worn last night, which were draped over the ladderback chair he sits in when he practices guitar in his room. He fished his key ring out of a pocket, shuffled to his dresser, and fit a small key into one of the drawers up top.

"What's with the tight security?" I asked. Someday, I was going to have to grill him about his paranoia. I wasn't sure it didn't have something to do with the weed I was suspecting he was smoking.

"Do you want to look at it in here?" Nick asked.

Snapshots

"No, I want to look at it in my room." I didn't state the obvious question, *What is it?* I knew the contents of the packet must have something to do with the letter I'd found.

I didn't know how much more strange and disturbing information I could take but whatever it was, it was going to be on my own terms—on my yoga mat.

"Do you want me to come with you?"

"No."

"Okay. Well, does the lock on your door work?"

"No, you know that." Dad had busted it one night a few years ago, when Macy and Sarah and I had locked ourselves in while sneaking makeup, which was totally against house rules. I'd had to bring Jilly and Aunt Margot into my campaign to wear at least a little makeup when I turned fourteen.

I actually don't know how Nick got away with his padlock, but Dad evidently decided to leave him alone. Nick and Dad had always had a cagey, wary relationship like they were sizing each other up and figuring out what the other would do next. It was the opposite of Dad's and Jon's chumminess.

"Oh, that's right. Well, I'll be here."

"Okay, thanks. You look really tired. You should go back to bed."

I took the packet. It was heavier than it looked, though it seemed to be stuffed with paper.

I went back and lit the new aromatherapy candle I'd bought at Candleabra in the mall. It was called French Peony. I didn't know what it meant, aromatherapy-wise, but it smelled so heavenly that it made me want to crawl right into the jar and sink into the wax.

Carefully, I poured the contents of the packet onto my mat.

There were dozens of cards of various sizes and colors and smaller envelopes containing letters addressed to Jon, Nick and me.

I could hear Nick tuning up his electric guitar in his room as I tentatively slid a few cards out of their envelopes as if they might be booby-trapped and snap my fingers.

Most of them were little-kid cards: colorful birthday greetings with funny animals, manger scenes or frosty landscapes with smiling snow-people. There were a couple of long envelopes for those tall, funny cards you buy for older kids and adults. I noted that these were all addressed to Nick.

I peered closer at the address under Nick's name on one of the envelopes. It was local, but it wasn't ours. 1016 Martins Lane was the Scheins' address. Before I could fully process that bit of weirdness however, my attention shifted to photos that had slid out of some of the cards. As my eyes drifted over the images in the snapshots, I recognized a couple of them from somewhere deep in my memory.

In one, a pretty, brunette young woman held a baby girl about one year old. The baby, wispy haired with gray-green eyes that seemed too large for her face, clutched a soft toy with a chubby fist, dimples like mini-staples across her knuckles. The other hand reached for a tendril of the woman's hair.

The baby was me, of course. The picture blurred over as tears plopped out of my eyes. I knew this picture. I don't know how, but I knew it.

I continued to sift through the others.

There were more pictures of me I'd never seen or didn't remember seeing—mostly as a young baby. There were shots of Nick and Jon as babies and then preschoolers. In another, Nick and Jon stood side by side, holding up matching shirt-and-pants outfits, still stiff on white plastic baby hangers.

In one, we all three sat in a gray-walled room. I looked older, maybe two or even three. I was old enough to sit in a folding chair at a round table where we were arranged before toys that looked new.

Instead of playing with toys, I clutched a pillow.

Snapshots

It too was new—Winnie-the-Pooh and Piglet, vivid against the bright-white background. They were holding hands and each held a tiny cross-stitched flower.

14

Ghost

I went back to the pictures and began sifting through them. I opened a couple of cards and started reading more carefully. I plucked out a sparkly card with an ornately iced, pink Sleeping Beauty cake on the front. I opened it.

For a Sweet Princess Who's Turning 5, it said in ornate, embossed purple script. Inside it was signed in neat cursive—also purple: *To my very own sweet princess, Emily Amber. You're such a big girl! I hope you like this picture. I would love to see a new one of you sometime. With all my love, Mommy. P.S. Granddaddy & Gram too.*

Ghost

I drew out the photo tucked inside the card. The picture was of my mother, flanked by two smiling, elderly people. I realized they were her parents. That meant they were my grandparents.

Throughout my life, I'd only thought vaguely about my mother. She was barely a real person to me—a figure in a photo that was long gone. She was certainly not a "mommy."

She signed the card "Mommy."

I had no "Mommy."

But here she was. She lived somewhere real, not even an alternate universe. Maybe it was a place foreign to me, but it was a real place. She had a real life, which she might still be living with other real people. This had never occurred to me.

Now there was proof.

My eye caught another photo, an obviously more recent shot. The colors vivid and defined, and the photo paper crisp and white. The woman looked much the same, though a couple of deep lines creased her high

Ghost

forehead. Her long hair was a lighter brown, highlighted around her face with a few threads of gray. She wore the same radiant smile. And, she was still beautiful.

Beside her was not a small child, but a grinning teenage boy who towered over her.

It was Nick—not-long-ago Nick.

I could feel my heart rise in my chest. I looked up from the pictures toward my door, which was now reverberating with White Stripes riffs from Nick's room down the hall.

What was going on?

Then there was screaming.

It wasn't until Nick barged through my door, still wearing only pajama pants, hair sticking straight up, that I noticed the screams came from me.

"You... know her."

"Em, I'm just going to lay it out here as best I can, okay?"

Ghost

I rocked back and forth on the mat, unable to keep still.

"She sent all these cards and pictures and other stuff too," Nick said, sitting down beside me on the floor. "They got returned to her, see?" he said, pointing to one of the many envelopes marked *Return to Sender*. I noticed what was repeatedly on each envelope wasn't one of those stamps from the post office, with the pointing finger. The message was always written in precise black print and underlined twice.

Dad's handwriting.

"She saved everything, what she got back anyway and gave it all to me when we met," Nick said. "She said there was a lot more, and presents, and sometimes money she sent us. Most stuff was returned, some not. She hoped us kids, you and Jon and me, at least got some of it."

I wanted to ask who'd sent the stuff back to her unshared with us kids, but I knew who it was. I mean, he'd obviously sent them back himself. What was all this, and why? Where'd it come from? I felt like my head was about to explode.

I kept staring at the pile, trying to summon the courage to voice the next thing on my mind, something equally obvious but more manageable somehow.

"You know her," I repeated.

Nick didn't say anything.

"Why? How long? How..." Not only was this mountain of returned cards and photos baffling, it made no sense at all. It was like learning that Santa Claus wasn't real after years of guessing, after people had chided you for having bought into it. After years of shame for only half-believing.

"I wanted to tell you. I didn't know how you'd feel, how you'd take it. I knew Jon wouldn't go for it. He'd just get pissed and tell Dad. And Dad...." His jaw tightened.

"Dad *what*?" I asked, my voice coming out sharp.

"Em, this might be hard for you to hear, but Dad's the reason we haven't known Mom all these years.

Ghost

She didn't go away on her own. When they were getting divorced, Dad went for sole custody. I think he knew people with influence at that courthouse, people who took his side and made sure he got what he wanted which was to get rid of Mom.

"She appealed the decision to give Dad sole custody every time. The judge kept ruling against her though. For no reason at all, they'd only give her supervised visitation. She would do anything to see us, but they kept making it harder and harder for her."

I tried to take one of my *pranayama* breaths, but it got pinched off somewhere in my chest. I realized both my hands had flown to my heart, as if I was trying to protect it.

"Then Dad moved us here from Atlanta, which was six hours away, and they made things impossible for her to get to all her visits. They blamed her for not being able to do it, to get here every time and to pay all of the travel expenses and court fees. Here's an example: the court ordered her to pay child support to Dad, but it had

Ghost

nothing to do with her income. It was too high for her to possibly pay. She also had to pay for her trips here and then she had to pay to see us at the supervising place. She lost her job due to being gone so much and she had to move in with her parents. She appealed again for a modification but had to pay for her lawyers. They even made her pay for her own mental exam, which was a total crock. They eventually cut off all her visitation and contact because she couldn't do all this crazy impossible stuff."

"She could have come anyway," I said stubbornly. "Tried harder. If I had my own baby girl, I'd never let anyone keep me from her. I'd go… hide somewhere with her. Like, until the court did the right thing."

Nick ran his fingers over the pile, chose a picture, and pulled it out. He handed it to me.

In the photo, we three kids and our mother were sitting on folding chairs at a card table in a sparsely furnished, dingy looking room. I could see a palmetto tree outside one of the windows. It was the same room as in the other picture with me holding the Pooh pillow. I was younger here though and sitting on my mother's lap. Jon and Nick looked tiny in their chairs, like the chairs were about to swallow them up as they tried to play with the toys on the table.

My mother was wearing overalls and a t-shirt and her hair was pulled back into a ponytail as if she'd come to play. A woman in a blue uniform sat a few feet away. She didn't look particularly threatening or anything. She was just staring straight ahead as if she had no connection whatsoever to us. She looked like a prison guard. Maybe she was.

"That's the visitation center. It was on Sullivan's Island, but it's gone now. There are lots of them all over the place, though. Those centers are set up for visits between parents without custody and their kids. They're mandated by the courts, but they're supposed to be for certain issues like when the court thinks a parent could possibly kidnap the children or the parent has a violent history."

"They thought our mom would kidnap us? Or hurt us?"

Nick shook his head. "Not really. Not in my opinion. But Dad's side must have convinced the court of that. Or worse."

"What's *worse*?"

"They planned for this to happen this way all along. They set Mom up. I'm sure of it. That's why we don't know her. Uh, why you and Jon don't know her," Nick corrected.

I grasped for something concrete, some *evidence* of some kind. Something real. I grabbed one of the tall card envelopes. "Okay, so why are you getting stuff sent to the Scheins?"

"Mom can't send stuff to me here for obvious reasons, so she sends it there and Scotty gives it to me at band practice."

Ghost

"You know her!" I realized I was repeating this same thing over and over, but somehow it seemed to take on more meaning each time. "How can you *know* her?" I stood up. My legs were sore and stiff. I folded into a forward bend. The picture of Nick with our mother caught my eye again. I held it up. "Okay, so—not that I really care—but when..."

Nick looked sheepish and sly at the same time. "You know that band camp I've gone to the last three summers?"

My mouth dropped open. "Nick...no!"

His impish grin said it all.

"People don't just lose their kids over *nothing*." Even as I loud-whispered this to Macy on Skype, I realized I sounded shrill, just like Sarah had on this very subject and sounding just like her mom. But it's the only thing that made sense. "She had to have done *something*. All that stuff Nick told me seems..."—I groped around for the right words—"like a really lame excuse."

Ghost

"There was a girl you talked about on your site," Macy said. "You told me her mom stopped coming to see her. I mean, if you ask me, this story doesn't sound so different from what some of your members talk about. If you don't mind me saying. Hey, do you want to come over? We can order out from Bread Baker's. I'm dying for soup. Something… hearty. Like split pea. This weather has me chilled to the bone."

And her with a freezerful of perfectly delicious bread from Faith Foods. I tried not to laugh. My friends were just as complicated and conflicted and confused as I was.

But as usual, Macy made a good point. I had my computer open so I clicked on the community shortcut and then scrolled back to the first community comments.

QUEENOFPINK: *My mom stopped coming to see us when I was 6. Now and then me and my sister try to find her but she never gets back to us. We've always wondered if we did something wrong.*

"She just didn't try hard enough," I said, more to QueenofPink—and to myself—than to Macy. "She should have moved here. Done something. What Nick said… that is so messed up and wrong."

"But see, it doesn't seem like she wasn't allowed to. Nick said she was behind in child support. She couldn't see you or she'd be arrested for violating the court order. Emily Amber, it just looks like a Catch-22. I mean, not to be on your dad's case, but what about the kids on your site? Don't some of them say the same thing?"

"Hey, whose side are you on?"

"Your side, Emily Amber. I'm always on your side. You know that."

"Nick and Dad have never gotten along," I said, hoping to find some way through this new pile of evidence which Nick had taken back to his room. Except for the Sleeping Beauty card, which I'd tucked under my yoga mat when he wasn't looking. "I mean… Dad wouldn't… Maybe she violated the court order by

Ghost

sending everything. I'm sorry. You'll just have to see this... stuff."

Now I understood why Nick was hiding it so diligently.

All the cards and pictures gone again, back in their drawer. Cards sent over many years. Cards and letters from a ghost.

Only it was beginning to dawn on me that maybe my mother wasn't the ghost, wasn't the one missing.

Maybe the ghost was me.

15

Log-Off

JEREMY21: Cool song choice. Fits great here. I don't know if you know the origins of your theme song, but I thought you'd enjoy reading about it.

He'd cut and pasted a Wikipedia entry.

SOMETIMES I FEEL LIKE A MOTHERLESS CHILD

This frequently recorded African-American spiritual dates back to the era of slavery in the United States. Children of slaves were often taken away from their parents. They were sold separately. The song expresses the despair and pain of this cruel, forced separation.

Log-Off

There are several interpretations of the song. One is that it shows the hopelessness a child feels who has been torn from his or her parents. But some have referred to the repetition of the word "sometimes" as a possible element of hope. It suggests that at least other times, a child might not feel motherless.

The "motherless child" could be a slave longing for his or her homeland, or motherland, Africa, hence the words "'A long ways from home.'"

Underneath, a sketch depicted what appeared to be a slave family being auctioned off. We'd studied the Civil War and the brutality and cruelty of slavery at school, of course. Charleston itself is practically a monument remembering the practice, such as the old Slave Market downtown, where crafts—not people—are now sold. These crafts include sweetgrass baskets made by artists whose careful fingers seem to remember the old ways.

I had never thought of slave families as such. I mean, I knew they existed, but it never occurred to me that the families were separated as if they'd never had the right to consider themselves a family at all. It was a horrible, unspeakably cruel practice.

I read the Wiki passage again. Despite how they were treated, these children of slavery had mothers—whether they were children or adults—and a motherland. The mothers lived on, as did the children. But most remained separated for life, ripped apart as if their relationships didn't matter. Worse, it was as if they were considered incapable of *having* relationships, like animals whose young are whisked away at birth and either sold or given away.

I thought of the confusion and sorrow of those children, watching their parents being examined as if they were animals and then sold off and led away. Did they know they'd likely never see one another again?

Then I considered how those parents and the rest of their families must have felt, desperately missing their children and sick with worry day in and day out. Wondering if anyone was being kind to them, if they had enough to eat, if they were ever given anything special. If they were being hurt.

I knew I didn't live in a world so terrible and punishing as that of slaves. I mean, look at me. Here I look at a pile of wonderful food, and instead of being grateful for it, I size it up to see if it'll cost me an unwanted pound or two. The closest thing to a job I have? Grocery shopping and saving money at Thrift-Eze.

But at the same time, I realized those words "Sometimes I feel like a motherless child" did pertain to me and lots of my community members too, much more than I'd thought. Our lives continued apart from our mothers, or fathers in cases like Lance B., and the bond was forever broken.

I was not really a motherless child, not anymore.

I never was. Just like my theme song said, I felt like one.

I hadn't heard from Bright in several days and I was starting to worry. I wanted to see how he was, tell

Log-Off

him all that had happened on my end, show him my new haircut. I'd gotten bangs. Despite all the angst that went into that decision, I wasn't sure I liked them even though Sarah and Macy both insisted I looked just like Rashida Jones.

The number I'd had for Bright was no longer in service, which hadn't surprised me because I knew he switched phones often. He'd withdrawn from the community too, but I knew that was just a safety measure as well. He might drop back in. Besides, the community project was going to be over in a couple of weeks.

I checked his YouTube channel. There was nothing new.

In a normal world, I'd assume I'd been dumped. In Bright's world, it was impossible to say. Plus, we were friends—not boyfriend and girlfriend even though he'd started calling me "babe."

Either way, I missed him.

Log-Off

Mr. Neil flagged me down on my way out of Life Skills on Monday.

"We were able to track your party crasher BostonBaked," he said. "They backed up all his comments and activity. He's in Massachusetts, obvious from his handle."

"Who is he though?" I asked.

"His name is Albert Swanson. And this isn't about me, but let's just say from my experience in my divorce, it helped me recognize this joker's rhetoric from the get-go. He put so much effort into throwing the mothers and kids under the bus. Trolls like BostonBaked make a full-time job of recruiting guys like me, who are divorcing, so they can target their wife and kids. They get government funding for representing and helping fathers get custody of their kids. They seem to spend the rest of their time harassing kids or women who talk about the situation. They dropped me like a hot potato when they saw I was going to be fair to Alicia and our girls. There's no money in fairness. Alicia and I are settling out of court with a mediator. I'm going to be even poorer, but I can hold my head up and know my kids are going to be okay. Alicia too."

He seemed to catch himself. "Sorry about that. It's hard to separate work from real life sometimes."

"I'm sorry, Mr. Neil," I said. "About your divorce and all."

"Well, thank you, Emily Amber. For better or worse, it seems I'm in right good company."

"Are they going to do anything? To BostonBaked I mean?" I was worried about further damage to my community. Posts from my members had dropped off since BostonBaked challenged just about anything they said.

"He could face hacking charges and maybe even harassment. Yours is the first community site that someone's crashed outright. There's a tighter firewall up now because of it. The students' work shouldn't be able to be accessed, much less trolled and ridiculed, like he did yours. It's a serious security breach and I'm sure it

Log-Off

was very difficult and daunting for you. Still, you did an excellent job."

He rummaged through his desk drawer and pulled out a paper sack. "Lunch time," he said. "Lucky me, I got the ten thirty a.m. slot this semester." He laughed a little, something he didn't do every day, in class, anyway. His teeth were straight and white, I noticed, except for one yellowed eyetooth.

"Is he... BostonBaked... gone?"

Mr. Neil nodded. "Yep. But this brings me to what I wanted to suggest to you. The Internet community project officially comes to a close in two weeks. We—Mrs. Park and Principal Landers and I— think it's best for you to go ahead and close out your site, given the circumstances. We don't want BostonBaked and his ilk, on our case.... Your case. He's being dealt with through other channels."

Mrs. Park is the guidance counselor, who everybody avoids except for absolutely necessary things like class changes. She's infinitely worse than Mr.

Log-Off

Landers. Mrs. Park has this creepy ability to detect stuff going on in your life. Macy says, "She reads your mail."

She means that figuratively of course but I found myself fingering the fabric letter in my down vest pocket. The letter was worn soft. I certainly didn't need Mrs. Park scrutinizing me right now.

"So tomorrow, how about we meet in the guidance office during homeroom," Mr. Neil said. "We'll help you tie up the loose ends."

I could tell it was already a foregone conclusion since the appointment was already set.

So it was going to be over. Just like that.

"One more thing before we go, Emily Amber. Did you ever tell your father about the project?"

I shook my head.

"Okay," Mr. Neil said carefully. "It might be time. I've felt all along that your project is your business and I felt your topic in particular took enormous courage. You handled everything beautifully, even as I'm sure you're

Log-Off

struggling with your own questions and concerns about your own life.

"But right now I'm pretty sure the school district will be looking at the assignment, and your project in particular, as a practical problem to solve. And for that, I am truly sorry."

JEREMY21: I see our "father-friendly" friend has gone. Looks like we're going to have to be super careful though. If he got on here, anyone could. It sucks.
SOULGRRL: Has anyone heard from Ember?
QUEENOFPINK: Oh no Ember, I hope nothing's wrong. But we're here for you!

I wasn't prepared for how it felt to look at my community for the last time. It wasn't like one of those school projects in which finally getting it done and handed in—or taken apart, like with the science fair—made you want to run and skip and call your friends. You're free.

You're so happy to have it off your back.

Log-Off

This wasn't like that at all.

I flexed my fingers, leaned over and typed:

Dear Motherless Child Community Members: I am so thankful for your support and sharing. I think we were able to help each other. I feel like I've met some of the greatest people. My school has had an issue from that man who flamed us—I caught myself and deleted "flamed"—*who joined us, who thinks we're not being fair. I thought we were just telling it like it is, saying how our lives have been. My teacher agrees with me and all of us, but we have to shut down early. I hope we can get together somehow again. I'll never forget you all. You helped me sort out some big things in my life.*

You won't be hearing from me again, on here anyway. I will always think about you. I want everyone to be safe and happy. And your parents—your mothers and fathers too—because whether they are alive or around or not, they are still…your parents after all. One more time, I'm sorry this had to end so suddenly.

Sincerely, Ember

Log-Off

There were no messages left to approve, no IM's and no more threads. It seemed the community had already gone silent. I felt a deep emptiness. I felt as if I'd finally caught a piece of myself and held it for a time, only to have it float away again.

I went to the community controls area, toggled the "live" button site so new posts could not be made. It would be frozen in time. The school would be able to remove the sites for good when it was all over.

From my end, I could only watch it go dark.

16

Names

I opened a new window and automatically clicked to Bright's video channel, which was my new habit. It's all I had left of him.

There was a new video, which had been posted just the night before. My heart gave a little leap and I clicked. There was Bright, sitting not in his room, but in a darker space, with only a bare wall behind him.

His hair was longer than ever. It probably wasn't intentional, but with his dark-blond bangs grown out, he had that middle-parted "prince"-looking hairstyle that was getting popular—the one which I'd never thought had a chance of being cute. Now, of course it was.

Names

"Hola. Bright here, coming to you from Sunny Basement of a Friend, Nowhere U.S.A. Life on the run is sketchy and stressful as expected. But I'm eating and I have a place to sleep. And best of all, my dad is not here to make my life as bad as it can possibly be. That's why I'm here, of course.

"So yeah, I could be more comfortable but at least I'm safe for now. I'll be here until I get the orders to move. Maybe this time it will stick. For now, I have Kahn Academy online and my language lessons and thoughts of my friends.

"I hope to touch base in a more tangible way sometime soon but for now, I have something for you. I think this is a piece you may be missing, one you've been looking for. I hope so."

Was he talking to everybody, or just me?

Bright held up a sheet of white printer paper with spidery blue ink handwriting; pretty, for a boy. I had to squint to read it:

FamilyCourtThievesAtLarge.us

Names

Then he held up another page.

Find your name.

I opened a new window, rewound the video to get the website URL again, paused it and pulled up *FamilyCourtThievesAtLarge.us*. On the homepage was a description:

This site is dedicated to non-custodial parents who, through immense miscarriages of justice due to corruption in the family legal system, have been denied rightful access to their own children. Conversely, their children suffer, while lacking if not mourning a relationship with the parents who arguably love them more... i.e., the parents who have no legal strings to pull or refrain from trying in the best interest of their children.

I wondered if this was Bright's own site, or one on which he collaborated. The words sounded like him.

Find your name. My name? Anyone's name?

I scanned the site's links section to the right. A header caught my eye: *Stolen Children*.

I clicked. There was a long list of names with dates beside them. I scrolled through.

Names

About halfway down was this:

- *Jonathan Paul Ross, Jr.—last seen by non-custodial mother Lynne Bryce (Ross), 4/5/2002*
- *Nicholas Bryce Ross—information unknown or withheld*
- *Emily Amber Ross—last seen by non-custodial mother Lynne Bryce (Ross), 4/5/2002*

I felt my pulses throb in my wrists and neck as I pressed *play* on Bright's video again, wishing so bad I could call or Skype him right now and feeling helpless that I couldn't.

I watched him hold up the second sign again: *Find your name.*

Then another message:

Click. Love ya, babe.

Click? I went back to the names, which blared white on a black background. Jonathan's and my names were hyperlinked in neon green. I clicked on mine.

Up came another site, framed with a soft pink and coral design. *Motherswithoutcustodyworld.com*

Names

In the center were three curlicued ovals with pictures inside—studio-looking pictures. A sort of online cameo collection.

There were two toddler boys, each in an oval with one on each side of the page. One was fair-haired and the other dark. A baby girl occupied the middle oval. Her hair was a wispy sandy brown and her tiny mouth a perfect little "o." She wore a blue gingham puffed-sleeve dress with a snow-white pinafore.

I gazed at the little dress, wishing I had it here for my quilt.

"I see your topic is very personal," Mrs. Park said to me the next morning in the guidance office. I sat in one of the itchy blue chairs next to Mr. Neil, who must have gotten a sub or some other teacher to monitor his homeroom.

I was already cursing my decision to wear my kilt and yellow mohair sweater today. It made sitting here itchier, even through my tights. The kilt is a Scottish

Names

tartan from my family—red and green and blue. I usually only wear it to church and to the Highland Games which is a huge festival for people of Scottish descent.

Anyway, it was perfect for an occasion that didn't exactly come with a dress code. I felt like one of those defendants on the stand in some crime show like *CSI: Special Victims Unit*. You know, where you can tell their attorneys made them wear a suit or a nice dress to make them appear more innocent or sympathetic to the court. Except I chose my outfit on my own.

Somehow I'd been able to hold my emotions and thoughts and feelings together since finding my mom's website. Granted it was a shock—it brought my mother's life to the present—but just like Bright had said, it was a missing piece. I was grateful to have it. It made me feel less disjointed about the whole thing.

I wished I could tell Bright about it.

"And these kids—these situations... are so sad," Mrs. Park was going on. "Surely you must have felt uncomfortable having to moderate this yourself."

I shrugged. Being uncomfortable hadn't occurred to me much. I'd been starved for information related to the idea of motherless children. "I just felt bad for everyone else," I said.

"David Benson. Do you remember him?"

"Who?"

"He went by Bright." Mrs. Park was consulting the red faux-alligator notebook splayed in her lap, still calm and not interrogating or anything.

I just stared at her.

"We've been in touch with his school. His account has been removed from your community, but there's a record. His father has reported him missing. His high school registers him as having been absent for ten days. The police have been alerted. Do you know anything about this young man or his private life?"

Names

It occurred to me that although I knew roughly where Bright lived—which was Kentucky—I didn't even know the name of the high school he went to. We hadn't talked about school much.

I realized Mrs. Park and Mr. Neil were staring at me, waiting for me to say something. All I could do was just shrug. I could feel a pit of misery forming in my stomach.

"The reason this is so important, Emily Amber, is that this—your community and what has happened on it—has become a legal matter. You see, I've personally been contacted by more than just Bright's father. And, there seems to be some concern about these children inquiring about their mothers. It gets into custody and family law issues, you understand."

"Concern from whom?" Mr. Neil broke in. "Emily Amber had my approval on her topic. It was a good, solid idea. She doesn't know what happened to her own mother. Why shouldn't she question it? And as I recall, at least one of the young men on Emily Amber's site was inquiring about his father."

Mrs. Park's bright-coral lips spread into her trademark lukewarm smile. "It's not that, Mike," she said. "It's the situations of some of the children who joined the community. In several situations, there appear to be allegations of abuse. Child Protective Services will need to be notified. We have a duty to report potential situations of abuse. You know that."

"Well, yes, in the classroom, but…" Mr. Neil started.

"With the Internet and all the new avenues of communication, our duties seem to be expanding. Emily Amber, you're certain you don't know anything about David… er, Bright?"

I was about to ask whether it would be better for Bright if CPS would finally look into his case and maybe help him. Out of the corner of my eye, I saw Mr. Neil shake his head ever so slightly. Or I thought he had. It was enough to make me decide against saying anything.

Names

"Why would she know anything about Bright?" Mr. Neil asked instead. "You know, I'm concerned about the position all of this puts Emily Amber in. All she did was follow the assignment. And she did it with my permission. No one had a problem with it until her site was divebombed by a Fathers' Rights activist."

"It seems as if Emily Amber unwittingly put herself in danger with a Life Skills project I never completely felt at ease with."

"Penelope, you're never completely at ease with anything," Mr. Neil replied, then seemed to correct it by adding, "You know what I mean."

Mrs. Park maintained her pleasant expression. I don't see how she does it but it seems very useful.

The phone rang. Mrs. Park leaned over to check the extension. "Hang on," she said to us. She picked up the receiver of her shiny black desk phone. "Yes. Okay. All right. Send them in."

"Who else is coming?" Mr. Neil asked. "I thought it was going to be just us."

Mrs. Park sighed. "I'm afraid it's become a bit more than that."

There was a light rap at the door. I recognized the figure behind the frosted glass. It was Dad.

It wasn't until he strode in that I saw Joy was with him.

"Hello," Mrs. Park greeted them. "Please have a seat, Mr. Ross. And…"

Don't call her "Mrs. Ross," I thought automatically, as if that could be the worst scenario going on here.

Joy was as dressed up as she'd been in the restaurant that day, wearing the same pearls, only this time against a pastel peach suit which did nothing to soften her look. "I'm Joy Handler, Emily Amber's attorney," she said to Mrs. Park, ignoring Mr. Neil and me. "A Guardian ad Litem. That means…"

"I don't see why Emily Amber needs an attorney present," Mr. Neil interrupted. "This isn't a trial."

"I'm here for Emily Amber," Joy said. "And as an interpreter, if you will, for the statement you received from the Families United Foundation. It's a special interest group."

"I know it well," said Mr. Neil.

"All right. Let's just discuss the matter at hand," Mrs. Park interjected. "Mr. Ross, you said you had concerns about this young man, David Benson. Emily Amber claims not to know anything about him personally, or about his life other than what he's contributed to his community."

I turned to Dad. How did he know anything about my community and Bright?

For the first time since he'd entered Mrs. Park's office, he looked at me. I could see a little glint of triumph in his expression. "Your friend Sarah's mother, Belinda Goddard, informed me about your community... Oh, two, three weeks ago," Dad said smoothly. "Belinda said Sarah was concerned that you were getting involved with a very troubled boy."

Names

So Joy hadn't appeared at 64 Prince for brunch that day because Dad was nervous about my asking about the baby things. He knew what I was up to. Mrs. Goddard had told him.

And Sarah had told her. I felt sick to my stomach.

"Can we get to the purpose of this meeting?" Mr. Neil asked. "I need to get to my first period class. We're supposed to be starting review for final exams."

"Emily Amber, this is beyond my element here but now there seems to be a disagreement about whether you know anything or not about David Benson. You do need to speak up, dear. You have to tell the complete truth. The police will ask you."

"I'm going to be collecting info from Emily Amber's cell phone and her computer," Joy said. I noticed Mr. Neil's face was going pink with anger.

"That is up to you," Mrs. Park said. "All right, let's move on. Emily Amber, Mr. Neil tells me you've already shut down your site."

Names

I nodded. I just couldn't think of anything at all to say. This was getting to be too much to process.

"The school has the final task of deleting the community sites after the entire nationwide project is done," Mr. Neil said.

"So, it looks like you've done your job insofar as the school goes," Mrs. Park said. "That's good. One more matter is that the special interest group to which your uninvited guest"—Mrs. Park glanced at her notes—"BostonBaked—represents, has threatened to sue."

"Sue?" Mr. Neil's voice was on Loud now. "That guy had no right to be there in the first place! He crashed her site! He was there illegally. They are investigating him or supposedly they are. All right, I've had it. I've reached my limit here. I'm tired of them—the Fathers' Rights and their agenda—having the floor… even when they're not present. Or shouldn't be." Mr. Neil shot a look at Joy. "This project is, or was, about the kids and what makes them feel alone or unique. Emily Amber seized on a very impressive concept built around a perfectly beautiful song.

"And I think even Emily Amber was surprised by the popularity of her community and how much activity she had. All she's done is moderate posts. What they say is not her responsibility. And I've been on the forum often to see how it's progressing. It's impressive. I've not seen any kid on there acting inappropriately, given their situations.

"I have no idea why Emily Amber has to be stuck in this position when this... group... infiltrated her community. What they did was not legal. Why aren't they answering to those charges, instead of keeping this girl out of class?"

Joy said, "But Emily Amber's community isn't as innocent as it seems. It's spreading lies about the community of *fathers*—a real community that is highly respected by all except a bunch of disgraced women and their children."

"Wait one minute," Mr. Neil thundered. "Disgraced? Disgraced how?"

"All right, this is completely out of my realm of understanding," Mrs. Park said.

"These women have not accepted certain decisions about their being fit—or not fit, as the case may be—for parenthood," Joy said. "Then they perpetuate the notion that they were robbed of their children by complaining to their communities and worst of all, to their kids. And some of these kids become true-blue troublemakers."

"Are you referring to David Brightman Benson?" Mrs. Park asked, seeming to desperately cling to the only part of the conversation she understood.

"I believe he's one of them," Joy said.

"Miss…"

"Handler. Joy Handler."

"Have you seen Emily Amber's site? I'm still having a hard time… placing… what your business is here."

Names

"I never had the pleasure of viewing Emily Amber's site," Joy said. "All I know is what her father and Belinda Goddard have told me."

"What does Belinda Goddard have to do with anything?" Mr. Neil demanded.

"Belinda is an old and trusted friend," Dad spoke up. "She was a key witness in my custody trial... er, involving my three kids. Years ago."

"What does this have to do with anything now?" Mrs. Park looked as confused as I'd ever seen her.

"Because we have cause to believe Emily Amber, and her friend Bright, are seeking to make contact with Emily Amber's biological mother. And it is against the law."

Mrs. Park sighed. "All right, all right. This is all completely out of the jurisdiction of this school. For our part, I'm going to write a letter apologizing to the man with the BostonBaked handle about anything that offended him and to remove the lawsuit since the site has been taken down.

"Emily Amber, you will no doubt be contacted by the authorities and it's likely if they didn't already have you on their list Miss Handler will make certain that it happens."

Joy looked pleased. "It's my job. And this—this is why Emily Amber needs me as her legal representative."

"It looks to me as if you're here to make damn sure to arrange the need for it," Mr. Neil said, leveling an icy glare at Joy. "It's the business you're in, is it not?"

Joy stood. "I need to leave. I have an appointment. Jon, thank you for letting me accompany you. You procure Emily Amber's electronics for me and I'll take it from there. If the police call, you know to call me. Emily Amber is not to be interviewed without me being present. We need to assure her safety.

"Thank you, Mrs. Park, for graciously allowing me to be here."

"I can't believe you're doing this to these kids," Mr. Neil said, standing also. "What is unsafe is the threats this BostonBaked character made to Emily

Names

Amber's community. He trolled them after gaining unauthorized access. And here you are, Penelope, apologizing? Apologizing for what? A group of teenagers making a pompous, grown man feel uncomfortable and unheard?

"And the only threats these kids have now are caused by people like you, Joy. If this young man Bright left home, presumably he had good reason. So you're worried about his father and his school and not about him?"

"He needs to be returned to the home the court determined was best for him," Joy said.

I couldn't bear it any more. "His father abuses him!" I screamed. "He leaves because he can't get away! No one will help! The court doesn't help and no one will listen!

"Bright helped me! I don't know where he is, but I wish I did! You can ask me all you want. Even if I knew, I wouldn't tell, because I want him to be safe! He's the

Names

only person I know who knows anything or who cares at all!

"I know about her, Dad. I know about her. Her name is... Lynne. And I know she sent us stuff over the years, lots of it, and you... you kept it from us. You lied, Dad. *Lied*.

"You couldn't find a baby outfit of mine. You didn't even keep them. You threw my stuff away—just like you threw our mother away!

"You've lied to me all of my life. I hate you—and you too Joy—and Mrs. Goddard and Sarah who's not a friend. She's sorry and a liar.

"You all lie. All of you. All..."

I don't know how much time passed or how long I was yelling or talking or ranting or whatever it was that I was doing. But the next thing I knew, some other people were in the office and it had become so hot and crowded and... itchy... that I swooned.

Names

The next thing I was aware of was a bright-white room and a monitor buzzing gently beside me. A soft, faded green gown had been tied on my body and a tube hooked up to my arm.

Someone—I'm still not sure who—had called 9-1-1 because they thought I was hysterical. Maybe I was. The EMS technicians gave me a tranquilizer shot and carried me out of school on a stretcher. Macy is forbidden by me to speak of it or tell me who saw. I just can't handle it.

"Wow, they brought you to the psych unit," Macy said when she came to visit me during the four days I was in there.

I wanted to dig a hole in the reclining bed and hide there forever.

Macy brought a big brown paper sackful of my favorite Faith Foods, already heated up. There were whole wheat rolls and bagels with low-fat veggie cream cheese which I love and oatmeal raisin cookies.

Names

"Dad says eat up because you now have a lifetime supply." Macy paused. "Just you though."

"Tell him thanks a lot. This hospital food is horrible."

"I think this ward is horrible," Macy said with a shiver. "Does it scare you to be here? Like, do you worry somebody really crazy is in the next room?"

I thought for a moment. I looked around. At least there was a TV with cable. And my best friend. The gown could use some embellishment. "Actually, I'd rather be here than at home. I'm scared to go home."

"I think your dad will need to be on best behavior, if what I hear Mom and Dad talking about is true," she said. "I mean, this is all I know, but that's exactly what Mom said. 'Jon is going to need to mind his p's and q's because people are watching.'"

I let out a huge groan. "Who's watching? No wait, don't tell me. I don't want to know. Macy, you have to promise me that if I beg you to tell me who's watching,

Names

and who was at school when they—took me out—that day you can't. I am not in my right mind, okay?"

Macy shrugged. "If you say so. It's not as bad as you think. Except for…" My heart sank. I held up a hand in warning.

"Ooh, hey, get this," Macy said to change the subject. "Guess who is a total vegan fraud."

I sat up a little straighter.

"Yesterday at lunch I saw Sarah—she was sitting with Jenny Mullins and Katelyn Andrews—and she was opening a package of Real Organic Cheese Slices!"

"Seriously?"

"I passed her on purpose on my way to the lunchline just to see what she was doing and she was going on about how she's a 'cheagan' now."

"A what?"

"Sam and I looked it up. A 'cheagan' is somebody who primarily eats a vegan diet but who cheats sometimes. Like Venus Williams, the tennis player.

Which isn't bad or anything, but when you're preachy like Sarah and her mother…"

"Have you ever tasted vegan cheese?" I interrupted.

"No. Why on earth would I do that?"

"I tried Cheez Pleez at Sarah's once. It tasted like stinky feet."

We laughed until my stomach hurt.

That seems like forever ago. I was only in the hospital for those four days, but pretty much like Macy had said, people were really careful around me when I came home. Like really, really careful.

Joy had tried to see me in the hospital, but the nurse on duty made her leave when I told her I had no idea who Joy was. I thought that was hilarious. Maybe I was still acting a little crazy, or maybe it was the meds, but I got a huge kick out of that.

Names

Dad came. Nick came (separately). Ashley came without Jon. I tolerated everyone. The sedatives and anti-anxiety meds helped.

Mr. Neil visited to tell me I'd gotten an "A" on the project and that mine was among only ten communities that received special commendations. "And keep up the good work," he added. "Never stop questioning. You deserve answers. You deserve to know about your life."

I thanked him and told him I hoped things were going okay for him after his divorce.

"It's okay. Bit lonely, but I see my kids a lot and my ex-wife and I are figuring things out."

I couldn't believe Mr. Neil and I were having such an adult conversation.

The Scheins sent me lovely Gerbera daisies, multicolored, in this cool purple vase. Mrs. Park sent me a cookie bouquet. Which was nice except it proves that she doesn't know me at all. I gave it to Nick to share with the Wingnuts at practice.

Names

When I got home from the hospital, I found my old phone was gone but that Dad had gotten me a new iPhone. I customized it with some new apps and added a ring tone of Grace Bobber singing "Let It Go" from Frozen. I know that song is totally overdone these days, but I like her singing it. She's near my age. It's a reminder to not worry, to just keep going.

I got my laptop back, but all my downloads and probably my whole hard drive had been erased. I didn't really care. I knew I could find almost anything again except my community.

As for my community, it felt far away, like a friend who suddenly moved in the middle of the school year. Like, I missed them all and still do. I hope they're okay, but every new day brings more things to do and to worry about. Everyday life just kind of takes over.

I could tell the kids at school were trying to act like nobody had seen me wheeled out of there on that stretcher. Or so I imagined. I only hoped the EMS techs

Names

or whoever sedated me did it before people figured out that I'd been the person screaming in Mrs. Park's office.

And Morris Fletcher asked me out. He goes to Cross Path Community Church. He's cute and apparently he considered me not too crazy to date, which I appreciate very much right now. Plus, I needed something to do, particularly when school let out for the summer. Macy had Sam Collins and I wasn't keeping up with Sarah anymore. Sometimes out of the corner of my eye I'd see her looking at me. I noticed she'd stopped wearing the silly mood ring, but that was only because I still sat catty-corner from her in Life Skills.

I know I can't blame Sarah completely. I know how Mrs. Goddard is and how she pries stuff out of Sarah. But if Sarah so easily sides with her mother, who is in the top five on my shortlist of people not to trust under any circumstances, then I know I can never trust Sarah again. Trust is essential to me now.

But I still miss Sarah. She was my oldest friend. I wish we could have finished our quilts together. I never found stuff to start one. And, even though the communities are long gone, I wonder if Sarah finished hers and how it turned out. Probably gorgeous. I thought maybe I'd look her up on Pinterest and see if she posted a picture.

There was a lot more to Sarah's and my friendship than what happened that last month or so. But these events somehow seemed to cancel out all the rest.

Shout

Have you ever experienced a time in your life when something bad happened like, you did something embarrassing or you were suddenly unpopular or maybe someone dumped you? You feel numb for a while or for as long as it takes to get over what happened? You can't imagine things will ever change or will ever get better?

But then one morning, you wake up and you're fine. I mean, you're more than fine. You don't feel sad anymore. You don't feel confused. You just feel plain *good*—good in your own skin like you're glad to be you.

Shout

Well, that's what I feel like today.

The morning sun sprays into my room and I can tell by the shimmery orangey-yellow color that it's already hot out. I lie in my bed a while and watch the sunbeams play on the walls. I've been thinking about repainting my room with a two-tone combo or even painting each wall a different color, mostly just to change things up. But the Honeysuckle looks so cool. I love feeling as if I'm in a bath of rose-colored light. Maybe I won't change it after all.

I don't even mind how hot it gets today. It's the Fourth of July, and there's the Scheins' annual party to look forward to. And, everyone's going to be there. Well, nearly everyone. Nick and his new girlfriend Carine, who is quiet but smart and pretty in her own ballerina way, and me, and Macy and Sam, and Jon and Ashley—only because Ashley insisted, she told me—and the Scheins' many friends of course.

Shout

My sort-of boyfriend Morris is at Edisto Island for his own family's reunion barbecue. He's bummed because he sees most of them all the time anyway and I get the feeling that he likes me a lot more than I like him. Which could actually prove to be tricky later on.

I'll bet you're wondering about Bright. I wonder about him too. I continually check his YouTube channel and I can't figure out where he is which is exactly what he needs I guess. But since my calls are being monitored, it's best to play it safe. Right now, it's just too dangerous. I know I kind of got off easy where he was concerned because of my breakdown or whatever it was. The police never interviewed me, but I had to sign a statement saying I didn't know anything about Bright's whereabouts.

Nick also asked me a couple of times—very carefully, like he was kneeling on cracking ice or something—if I might want to meet our mom sometime over the summer. I told him I'd think about it. So far I haven't. Thought about it I mean.

Shout

"I wouldn't know what to say or how to act around her anyway," I told him. "It would be weird."

"You'd just be yourself," Nick tried to explain. "She knows that the two of you haven't had a relationship over all this time. She'd just kind of like to say hello and maybe get to know you a little. That's what we did when we met, and it's gotten really cool."

It was all well and good to know she existed. But *meet* her? It simply seemed out of the realm of possibility—like when you draw a Venn diagram, and some of each circle intersects. Maybe Nick could fit comfortably in that middle area, but I felt like I was doing okay on the edge of my circle.

"I guess I just feel like I don't want to deal with all that right now," I said. "You know, after what happened with my project and all."

And that was that. And this is today.

I'm perusing the contents of my closet.

I seldom plan outfits in advance, although I might run through a few scenarios in my head. It's a

Shout

good five minutes before I pull out a navy denim skort and a cute red and white striped tank top I found at Thrift-Eze last week. Normally, I don't enjoy walking around looking like a human flag and I'd never put blue and red together. But, it's the Fourth of July after all.

I tie my white scarf around my head, pulling back my bangs, which I'm trying to grow back now. *Note to self: If you're not sure you really want bangs, then by all means do not get them.*

The Scheins have a pool, so I'm taking my new storebought turquoise Billabong fringed bikini and a cute matching sarong. I draw my thrift-shopping line at swimsuits, nightgowns, and underwear.

Nick is putting the big Lands' End cooler and stuff in the Volvo. He's wearing the plaid Bermuda shorts and navy Lacoste shirt I found for him at Thrift-Eze. It's his Wingnuts "uniform." Wearing it, he looks completely unlike himself, which is what the Wingnuts go for. He says they look preppy to be ironic, like the band Weezer. I think they look just like everyone else in

Shout

the bar or the restaurant or wherever they're playing, but whatever.

Today, the Wingnuts are playing at the Scheins' party, so Nick's also got his amp and guitar and other stuff to load in. I'm going to balance our party offering—which is a fishmold complete with olive-slice and pimento eye—on my lap. I found the recipe on *Lo-Fat and Flavorful*.

I guess Jon has already gone to pick up Ashley. Dad's golfing with Mr. Rutledge and some other people like he always does on the Fourth.

Nick and I finally get in the car which is hot even though it's been in the garage. I welcome the rush of air on my face as we ride with the windows down to Carine's house a couple of miles away. Then we stop by for Macy, who comes out of her house bearing a huge bag of Faith Foods hamburger and hotdog buns. Her parents are going to the Cross Path picnic, where Faith Foods always has a big booth. According to Macy, Sam's mom is making him go to their picnic too ever since her

Shout

spiritual epiphany and she joined Cross Path, but that he will catch up with us at the Scheins' later.

The Scheins' driveway and half the block each way in front of their house is already crammed with cars. We step out into heat steaming off the asphalt in shimmering waves, and to the sweet scent of fresh gardenia and honeysuckle. I can hear shouting and music from here.

Nick and Carine and Macy and I get most of our stuff out of the car and Nick leaves the windows down since anything of value is in our arms. We make our way to the Scheins' house. It's a rambly brick ranch on a large, impeccably kept lot. They live in Mount Pleasant, which is not as stiff a historic district as downtown Charleston. We enter through the back gate to where the party is.

First I have to stop by the tent where the food is being set out. I peel the plastic wrap off the fishmold and arrange a fan of table water crackers around the edge of the plate. It's an appetizer, which means it can be eaten whenever people get hungry.

Shout

Macy and I then head straight for the cabana which always smells heavenly, like freshly shaved sandalwood. I'm forever looking for aromatherapy candles that smell like it but I haven't found the perfect match yet.

I quickly change into my swimsuit since my red white and blue outfit is more for the barbecue this evening. That's when the fireworks are set off and I actually feel responsible for looking patriotic. Macy's wearing this boldly striped caftan thing over her swimsuit that makes her look like an African warrior princess. She seems to have switched out her atheism kick for a cultural identity phase. Also, she's grown about five inches this past year and now she towers over me.

We score a couple of lounge chairs right beside the pool. Macy's grabbed us some cold canned lemonade from one of the coolers scattered throughout the yard. Kids are already splashing around in the pool, which is styled to look like a grotto. We drag our chairs out of the

Shout

way just enough to miss the general horseplay and stay in the rocky section, which gives the impression of cool even if it isn't.

"Hey, I'm joining my church Sunday," Macy's telling me as I smooth Banana Boat sunscreen to all the parts of myself I can reach.

I'm genuinely shocked. "What made you decide that?" I ask, squinting at her like she's sprouted a second head.

Macy shrugs. "I don't know, I still don't think one particular religion actually gets it all. But, I like singing in the choir anyway, so it's not like I can go somewhere else on Sunday mornings, you know?"

I hand her the sunscreen and she shakes a blob into her hand. "Wow, pungent," she says, wrinkling her nose. "And... Sam will be there, of course, with his mom's religious experience and all. She insists he go there with her. Sam's dad is Catholic though. It's causing tension in the home from what I understand."

Shout

"Oh wow." I hadn't gone to church with Macy the past couple of weeks though I usually try to lately. Ashley and I have stayed up really late the past couple of Saturday nights, which are the only completely free evenings she has. She's totally joined me on my mission to give our whole house a Feng Shui makeover. Dad's been giving me such wide berth—as if he's afraid of what I might do—that I've been allowed to do practically anything. Within reason I mean.

Anyway, Ashley and I decided to start by ditching the dirty living room carpeting with its exposed staples and replacing it with the kind of wood laminate flooring you can press in yourself, sort of like a giant puzzle.

As Macy and I sit side by side with legs outstretched in the sun baking warm but not unbearably hot yet, I can't imagine being happier *anywhere*. We sit mesmerized, taking in the shimmering green surface of the pool.

Shout

Over in this little arbor-type area across the yard, the Wingnuts are tuning up. I can make out through a curtain of wavy heat that Carine has seated herself on a nearby low stone wall. Her long, light brown hair is twisted into a loose braid over one shoulder. Unlike Ashley, she's quietly attentive to what Nick is doing but she's her own person too. I watch her slide a small book out of the large batik beachbag she's brought.

And I just love her even more. She's not around a whole lot because she's a dancer and she spends most afternoons and evenings at the studio. Then she has her homework to do. It all works out rather perfect with Nick's schedule. They mainly see each other on the weekends and they're good with that.

"Hey, who do you think is cuter, Scotty or Adam?" Macy asks lazily, and we embark on our annual debate about the Schein boys.

The Wingnuts start their set with one of their best songs, "If I Were a Minotaur." Their genre has changed about six times since they formed and is now what Nick calls *folk metal*. As best as I can figure, it's a blend of history and mythology played real hard and loud. He says they dress the preppy way they do to make a point.

What the point is exactly I'm not sure. It's definitely weird to see these guys dressed like they're going golfing, rocking out in a confusion of loud wailing instruments and lyrics you find yourself trying to pick apart long after the song's over. And then there's Adam with his newly acquired accordion thrown in the mix… Well, you'd just have to hear them to know what I'm talking about.

We watch groups of kids playing horseshoes and Frisbee until the sun starts getting to Macy and me. We decide to go inside to cool off, use the bathroom and freshen up. Sam's due to arrive within the next hour or so and Macy wants to look just right.

The Schein house is one of those in which you can go just about anywhere and nothing seems off limits. They expect you to make yourself comfortable, so you do.

Shout

We go in the sliding glass door that leads into the basement because their house is on a slant. This is rare as Charleston doesn't have many hills. This is also what makes their house look so much bigger on the inside than it does from the outside. It strikes me how different the basement looks in the daytime, with the sunlight pouring in. I've spent many evenings here at band practice lately, when I'm not with Morris or Macy. Nights are shadowy and cozy here.

I can't bear to be in our house alone if there's a chance Dad might linger. I get the impression that he feels the same way.

We blink the sun out of our eyes and let them adjust to the indoors, basking in the cool for a few moments. We use the basement restroom, but then go upstairs as soon as we hear country western music playing on the stereo upstairs. I instantly recognize Patsy Cline. I became kind of obsessed with her after watching that movie Coal Miner's Daughter.

Shout

"Well hello, girls," Mrs. Schein says. "I didn't realize you were here yet. Then again, I haven't stepped outside of this house all day." She's standing at the kitchen counter, setting cupcakes on a tray while a lady whose brown hair is swept up in a seafoam green scarf spreads white icing on each of them. Scattered on the table are little American flags which I imagine will adorn the cupcake tops.

"Hi Mrs. Schein," Macy and I say. "Thanks for having us."

"You are beyond welcome," Mrs. Schein says, flashing a smile. I notice she's gotten braces on her teeth.

The other woman appears determined to frost the cupcakes to perfection. She holds one up and peers at it as if she's trying to find a flaw. I notice her fingers are pale and slender—like a concert pianist's—and painted the palest pink. She looks vaguely familiar, but I can't place her. She could be the mom of any one of the kids here.

Shout

We go to investigate the family room, from which we hear lots of laughing and yelling. We hang a bit watching Pete Kennedy and a bunch of his friends play Fallout 4 until we get bored and decide we've cooled off enough to go back out to the pool.

As we go back through the kitchen, Mrs. Schein has disappeared while her friend is sticking a flag on top of each perfectly iced cupcake.

"Those look really pretty," I say, and she kind of half looks up at me and smiles but she's still deeply absorbed in her decorating. I don't think I have that much perfection in me and that's saying a lot.

I stand there studying her for a few moments trying to place her, but Macy's pulling me along to get back outside.

The Wingnuts have finished their set and Nick has gone to sit beside Carine. They have their heads together talking. Carine has a soft voice that you really do have to lean in to hear. But they stop talking and

Shout

break apart when I walk up as if they'd been sharing some kind of a secret.

Out of the corner of my eye I can see Ashley in the pool, hanging onto Jon like he's a life preserver and she's drowning.

Macy skips off to get us a plate of appetizers. "I'll check on your fish mold to see if people are biting," she says and winks. I have to laugh at her attempt to make a joke.

"No PDA, okay?" I say to Nick and Carine. "This is a family affair. Plus, it's majorly embarrassing." Nick grins back but doesn't remove his arm from Carine's slender shoulder. For some reason, I just love this.

"Are you having a good time, Ember?" Carine asks. She's picked up on my nickname because she hears Nick say it all the time. I'm not even sure she knows it's not my real name, which is cool. I'm actually thinking of going by Ember starting next year. That's if people catch on, I mean.

Shout

"Yeah, but it's hot. I don't think I want to get wet unless I have to."

Carine smiles. "Well, you look lovely wet *or* dry. Have fun."

I'm hoping Carine and Nick decide to marry young as I meet Macy at our lounge chairs. "Your fish mold has been majorly attacked," Macy tells me. "All that's left is part of the tail." She's piled a plate full for the two of us, featuring the last fish-scale of my mold, some cut up fruit and several enormous chocolate brownies.

I take a cracker with nothing on it and close my eyes, listening to the splashing and yelling going on in the pool. I hear Ashley's shrieks as Jon attempts to throw her and the murmurs of people walking around us.

I don't think I fall fully asleep but I'm lulled into a sort of daydream in which I'm trying to identify a blurry face. Moving in closer doesn't bring it into focus.

Toward the end of the day, the beating sun and the excitement of the holiday have worn the sheen off of

Shout

the party. Even the Wingnuts, having played much of the day in the heat, are now wilting. They've disentangled themselves from their instruments and have joined their friends in various phases of cooling off in the pool, scarfing down food at the food tent and watching TV inside.

Macy wants to grab the party outfit she left in the car, so I follow her down the pebbled walkway and across the freshly mown front yard. While she opens the car door and lets the hot air seep out for a minute, stepping from one foot to another to keep her bare feet from burning, I look around me and observe the summer twilight scene.

Then I spot Jon, who has chosen the same moment to go to his car for his cooler. Even though the Scheins have coolers all over the place, I suspect his contains his special brew, if you know what I mean.

I notice now that there's a knot of people on the front lawn standing under the enormous magnolia, which casts a dramatic shadow against the violet-blue

Shout

sky. I make out that it's Nick and Carine. They're talking with Mrs. Schein and the woman who'd been so painstakingly decorating the cupcakes, who has donned a pair of huge round white Jackie O sunglasses. I imagine she might be Carine's mother.

Jon walks by them slowly, giving them a hard look as he passes. I'm guessing he's trying to cop a good look at Carine, who stuns him silent when she's around. She's not around very much, so maybe that's why he's so enthralled by her.

We go back in and Macy disappears to put on her party outfit. I've decided I'm not bending to the red white and blue thing since there's plenty of that around. Plus, I feel super cute in my swimsuit. Although I'd long since hit size my goal of being a size 2, by the time I got out of the hospital I was a 0. My shrink says the anxiety meds I have to take help curb my appetite. Of course, she also says to not let that stop me from eating a balanced diet. You can probably guess that I view curbing my appetite as a huge plus, though.

Mr. Johnson, Lindsay Johnson's dad, is getting the huge grill ready. Like the pool, the grill has its own grotto. The aroma of firing charcoal magnetizes me. Maybe, I can recreate that charcoal smell with my own aromatherapy line. I'd include cedar cabana, freshly mown grass, honeysuckle and gardenia. I could call it the Southern Summer Evening Collection or something.

I plan on offering help to Mr. Johnson, but first I duck into the cabana and sneak a look at myself in the mirror. My cheeks are pink from too much sun, but otherwise I look okay. I dab on some lip gloss from my cosmetic bag and brush out my hair, which has matted with sweat around the temples. I dab pressed powder around my face and on the circles under my eyes. I notice my cheekbones have become more prominent.

I happen to pass Ashley and Jon, who are sitting at one of the small café tables scattered around the back

Shout

yard. I can tell they're trying to keep their voices down, but anger seems to hang above them like a wavy mirage.

"No, Jon, I'm *not* going to let you do it," Ashley says.

"Don't tell me what to do," Jon snaps. "I think he needs to know."

"Why? Why does he need to know?"

"Because. It's just… the right thing to do."

"It… is… not."

They continue to go back and forth and I walk away as quickly as I can. I'm not letting a silly argument—especially one that doesn't include me in any way—ruin my glorious day.

"I'm back," I say to Mr. Johnson and I set about opening new bottles of ketchup and mustard and uncovering bowls of sliced onions, tomatoes, and lettuce someone's already prepared. "Hey, have you ever tried mixing mayonnaise and onion soup mix in with the hamburger when you're making the patties?" I ask. "It's supposed to make them super moist. It's a recipe from

Shout

Trisha Yearwood. I heard her talking about it on the radio."

Mr. Johnson raises an eyebrow. "Hmm, sounds tasty. Ours are formed already, but I'd sure welcome you as sous chef next time." He smiles at me.

I feel sublimely happy standing here, arranging condiments by size and color, popping caps and twisting open jars. The warm summer air is infused with delicious grill smoke.

I love this time of night, especially at a party. The night is far from over, but people have settled in and everything looks different somehow. The pool is calmer, glittering under the overhead lights that someone has cut on a little early. Fireflies begin to show like tiny pinpricks of light suspended in the air a second before they disappear. Voices lower to a soothing hum. I don't even hear Jon and Ashley anymore.

There's a deep peacefulness about it, like the end of a good yoga session only here, everyone else is in on it too.

Shout

Then several loud voices pierce the stillness in a cacophony coming from the front yard. It sounds like people are trying to talk over one another. It's not Ashley and Jon either. It's not Ashley, anyway because she's sniffling by the bandstand, shredding and reshredding a paper napkin.

Someone bursts through the back gate and bellows, "*Where is she?*"

I look up from my condiment arrangement.

It's Dad.

Following him are Mr. Schein, looking upset and angry, Mr. Rutledge, looking bewildered and seeming to be just trying to keep up—and Jon, looking scared.

A woman in a red Hawaiian print sundress, who I don't know, is standing in the middle of the patio. Her mouth is open in an "O" of astonishment as a man in a matching flowered shirt yanks her out of the way.

"*Where is she?*" Dad roars again.

Shout

The party has stopped. Everyone's looking around at one another, wondering what Dad is talking about, who he's looking for. For a sickening moment, I'm afraid it's me. But even in this scary scene, when he's obviously off his rocker, I don't think so. I've never prompted a reaction from him like this, especially after my project was exposed and everyone went on good behavior.

Mr. Johnson knows my dad. "Emily Amber, why don't you go sit over there near the house," he says in a low tone, and watches while I do what he says.

Dad sees me anyway.

"Emily Amber, where is she?" he barks.

I haven't a clue what he's talking about. "Wh- Who?"

"Your mother. Go get her."

And here's where my world hurtles into space again because I have no earthly idea what he can possibly be talking about. It's like a crazy time warp. He

Shout

sounds as if he's returning home after a rough day, and Mom is somewhere in the house.

Mr. Schein steps in. "Jonathan, you're out of control," he says breathlessly. "You've been drinking and you're upset. There is nothing here for you. You need to leave." He reaches for Dad's arm but Dad snatches it away and rounds on Mr. Schein, who's at least half a head taller than he is.

The evening light is fading, but I can see Dad's eyes glowing white and wide and bloodshot. He looks like... He looks like a wild creature, not a person.

"She's my wife."

"Not anymore, Jonathan," Mr. Schein says. "Not for a long time."

The lights go on in and around the house and Mrs. Schein steps out of the sliding glass door holding a jug of tea in one hand. "What's going on?"

"Lilah," Dad says to her in a menacing tone which sounds more like warning than a greeting.

Mrs. Schein just looks at him.

Shout

"Where is she?" Dad demands again. He's planted his feet about a foot and a half apart and folded his arms across his chest like a bully cop.

"Who, Jonathan?" Mrs. Schein asks softly. She sets down the tea and wipes her hands carefully on her pink and green flowered Lilly Pulitzer skirt. But, I can tell by the way she seems to be gathering composure that she knows something.

"Jonathan," she says, "nothing Lynne does is your business. You did every single thing a person could do to drive her out of your life and out of the children's lives. You've no business looking for her here."

"She has no right to be here."

"How do you know that she's even here, Jonathan?" Mrs. Schein asks, amazingly calm. She sounds as patient as a kindergarten teacher comforting a kid on the first day of school.

My dad looks around and scans the crowd, and seems to spot my brother Jon sulking near where Ashley is. It strikes me that Ashley, who's usually hanging on

Shout

Jon like some kind of afterthought accessory, has seemed to scrunch herself as far away from Jon as she can without falling out of her chair. She looks miserable.

"My son informed me of it," Dad said, and everyone turns to stare at Jon. If there's a universal expression for horrified guilt, it would be what Jon's face looks like right now.

I'm beyond confused. This is not happening.

What is happening? Jon told Dad my mother was here? She's not here. She's… wherever she is. This has to be some colossal joke—some huge prank. I've been transported to an alternate universe where I'm suddenly living with a choice someone else made, which has led to a completely unexpected outcome. The rest of us are merely along for the ride.

Mr. Schein walks over to stand next to Mrs. Schein. "Well, that's neither here nor there. Now go home and sleep this off. Your kids are all here, we've all been having a really nice time…"

Shout

"I'll bet you have," Dad snarls, and starts poking around in the bushes near me, but Mr. Johnson is still standing in front of me.

A crowd has gathered now. People are obviously confused and curious but they know not to get close.

"Jonathan, don't make us call the authorities," Mrs. Schein tries to reason. "We have guests here. We don't want a scene. Please, just go on home."

Nick steps out of the house just then and I can see Carine and the brunette woman standing behind him—the one with the seafoam scarf who was icing the cupcakes so carefully. I notice she's still wearing the sunglasses despite the deepening twilight.

I look at them through the sliding door and I know who she is.

She's my mother.

"Dad, leave her alone," Nick says. He's clearly trying to be brave and take control of the situation but his voice cracks a little. Mr. Schein shakes his head at him

Shout

and signals Mrs. Schein, cupping his hand to his ear to simulate a phone call.

Mrs. Schein disappears back into the house.

My mother steps out. "Jonathan," she says simply, and pulls off her sunglasses, letting them dangle from one hand.

My dad stares at her. A ripple seems to pass over him like a hesitation or a feeling or something that temporarily covers his anger. Then he seems to harden back up.

"Lynne, what the hell…"

"I've a right to be here, Jonathan," my mother says as she looks him directly in the eyes. I notice she's taller than she looked standing beside Mrs. Schein. Her eyes almost line up with his. The green flecks in her eyes complement the scarf she's wearing. And they seem to sparkle with defiance.

"You. Do. Not." Dad's forehead is bulging with veins. This must be how someone looks before they have a heart attack or a brain aneurysm.

"Well, you made sure I couldn't have access to my children and you made sure I'd get thrown out of any public place—a ball field, a restaurant, a children's party. But this is a private party to which I've always been invited. The Scheins have been my friends ever since we lived in Atlanta."

"You have no friends," Dad says to my mother in a scorching tone, staring her down and reaching back as if he's about to take a swing at her. But, his arm freezes in midair as if he can't decide what level of force to use.

Nick rushes in and puts his arm around my mother's shoulders and tries to move her away from Dad. My mother stands firm— perfectly composed like a statue. She shakes her head at Nick, as if to say "No," but he stays there, the two of them locked in some kind of silent showdown or something.

People are transfixed, looking alternately from the scary scene between my dad, my mother, and Nick, and the back gate. I'm sure they're looking for the cops to arrive.

Shout

Suddenly my dad explodes. "Nick… You stay away from her! She's nothing but a whore and a liar and a… nutcase! She's not fit to be your mother! Or anyone's mother!" His face has gone so red that it literally looks like it's going to explode.

Nick says evenly, "Then why don't you tell us what she *did*."

Everyone is staring in disbelief. I'm still watching this as if from above like I'm watching some twisted family drama and I don't even know these people.

Dad blusters. "She… She… She was arrested for contempt of court."

Everyone's transfixed and as riveted to the drama as I am. While I'm shaken of course, or shocked or whatever, I'm not afraid for my own safety or anything. I realize that I'm somehow *bearing witness*. It's the only way I can describe it.

"Jonathan," my mother says softly, "it was after the final custody decree. It was at that moment I realized I'd lost my children. I'd worked my heart and soul out trying to save them. I'd spent every penny I had and every penny my parents had too. I'd followed all the rules—every last one of them. I'd trusted that truth would win out even after all the dirty games everybody was playing."

"Not games," my dad smirked. "Justice."

My mother shook her head. "There was no justice. Only money, power and cruelty. It struck me then after the judge made the ruling that I had lost… Everything… That I was done. And justice hadn't prevailed. Good hadn't trumped evil and greed. It was over."

"So what did you do? Tell everybody what you did. You showed your ass. You embarrassed yourself in front of the whole courtroom. Go on, tell them."

"I cried," my mom said.

And suddenly, I can't take any more. I have to get up, to move, to breathe. I rise and push myself past Mr. Johnson, who's never moved. Then, Mr. Schein, then

Shout

Dad, then my mother and then the lady in the Hawaiian sundress who's crept up again to get a bird's eye view.

I scan the yard for somewhere to go. I could go to the car, but it's not like I can drive away because Nick has the keys. I walk straight ahead and keep walking until the pool looms right in front of me, silky green and serene.

I step in.

The water is soft. There's a tingle of saline and I remember the Scheins have converted to a salt water pool. It's lovely, like swimming in a warm bath.

Like swimming in tears.

I dive under and swim downwards. Down. Down. I realize I'm still wearing my thong sandals and I reach down and pull them off as I swim, letting the shoes float up and away. I swim forcefully and determinedly to the bottom of the pool, where I touch down briefly before soaring back up for air in a cloud of bubbles.

I take a deep breath before ducking down again, because I don't want to be on the surface, up with the

Shout

crazy people. I want to be suspended here and free at the same time.

Swimming, I feel just like the character Alice who falls down the rabbit hole toward Wonderland and cries until her tears make a pool. Then after she shrinks, she has to literally swim in her own tears. She swims and swims just like I'm doing now. She passes a mouse, a duck and a Dodo bird floating by and I'm passing the Scheins' floating beer cooler...

I don't know how much time has passed. I swim and swim and float until my body is exhausted and without feeling at all, like I can now float up and away in one of my bubbles.

As long as I'm not up there on the ground, I'm okay. Because the ground is hateful and confusing and *hard*.

Finally, I draw up to the aqua tiles on the side of the pool and rest my head there. I let my body rise behind me and float, like I'm lying on a soft mattress of water.

Shout

Suddenly, I realize I've slid back and slipped under. But I've no energy to swim and my arms make no traction when I move them.

I'm lost. Lost in the water. I'm beginning to panic. I can't find my way up. My lungs are burning and my chest is cramping up. Fiercely, I try to paddle while cupping my hands like Lee, my old swim teacher, taught me. Where is the air? Where is up? Ice cream scoops. Strawberry, chocolate. Scoop, scoop.

"Emily Amber!"

"Ember!"

I'm dragged behind powerful strokes, hauled through the water and up into white-bright light.

Brick-hard heat. Pounding on my chest until a rush of air, blistering cold, roars through me.

A ring of blurs. I can just barely bring a face into focus. I try to peer closer but I'm looking into yet more sea green, into orbs that look ethereal, like they belong in the watery world I just left.

Shout

I'm looking into eyes that are deep, and beautiful, and... knowing. They know me. The kindness that flows from these eyes is indescribable. Maybe I've drowned or something. Maybe I caught myself on the drain or my arms suddenly forgot to keep paddling.

They say the feeling of love that envelops you when you die is beyond anything you can imagine. And even though I know I'm very much alive, I'm feeling that kind of love.

"Are you feeling better, Emily Amber?" a voice asks softly.

I think I kind of nod, but I'm too tired and out of it to tell.

This angel, or whatever she is, gently tucks a wet tendril of hair behind my ear and wraps me in a thick, sun-warmed towel. She pulls me onto a lounge chair with her and folds me in her arms. I look up and watch the stars gleam white against the soft black sky. It's as if they're guarding us.

And I sleep.

"Let the jury consider their verdict," the King said, for about the twentieth time that day.

"No, no!" said the Queen. "Sentence first—verdict afterwards."

"Stuff and nonsense!" said Alice loudly. "The idea of having the sentence first!"

"Off with her head!" the Queen shouted.

—Lewis Carroll, from *Alice's Adventures in Wonderland*

Acknowledgments

The authors wish to thank the following people who were immeasurably helpful in the writing of this book: Jenna Brooks, for finally convincing us the story wasn't finished and for her fierce belief in the addition of 20,000 more words; Kelly, who's been there through thick and thin and everything in between; Cousin Jerry for his humor and encouragement; Malinda Sherwyn and Rochelle Rigsby for providing wit and wisdom in the most nonsensical circumstances (a fresh round of napkins for the Bad Girls' Table, please!); Janie's mother Mary Patrick for reading every version and always saying it was good; all our friends, both Facebook and in the flesh, for their amazing ideas and moral support both in real life and this story; Josh and Paul for putting up with constant chatter about the book, and for their patience and meal preparation and respect for the project; our children both present and not present; and all the mothers and children who have been victimized by "the system"—may they find some comfort and hope and even some laughter in these pages. To all the children: We hope this book might provide some clues and answers, and the knowledge that you are not alone in your wondering; and at the very, very best, we dare to hope for mother and child reunions.

ABOUT THE AUTHORS

Janie McQueen

Janie McQueen is the author of five books, including Hanging On By My Fingernails: Surviving the New Divorce Gamesmanship, and How a Scratch Can Land You in Jail; The Magic Bookshelf; and its 10-year anniversary edition, The New Magic Bookshelf. She has been a reporter for major metro newspapers including The Greenville (SC) News and the Atlanta Journal-Constitution. A native of Beaufort, SC, she has a BA in English literature and writing from the University of South Carolina. She lives with her husband and four children in metro Atlanta. www.janiemcqueen.com

Robin Karr

Robin Karr's varied career includes working as a technical writer for USCIS Department of Justice, teaching high school English and working for more than thirty years in retail management. She has worked as a writer and activist for womens' and children's rights since the late 1980's. Robin holds a BA in English from Union College in Kentucky. Her oldest son Christopher—aka Critter—Karr is a writer who lives in Austin. Robin's two younger children Matthew and Laura were taken in babyhood by a Texas judge who was later ousted from her position. Her journey to make meaningful contact with them continues at www.motherswithoutcustodyworld.com.

Learn More

To learn more about this book, or for related information, resources, discussion and multimedia, please visit www.themotherlesschildproject.com.

Author Appearances

Both Janie McQueen and Robin Karr welcome the opportunity to appear at book signings, as media guests or interviewees, and as speakers for interested groups. Please visit this book's website at themotherlesschildproject.com, or the authors' individual websites, janiemcqueen.com or motherswithoutcustodyworld.com, for informatio